Lost & Found

Lost & Found

Karey White

Orange Door Press

ISBN 13: 978-1-941898-05-5

Published by Orange Door Press

The Ripple Effect Romance Series

Like a pebble tossed into calm water,
a simple act can ripple outward
and have a far-reaching effect on those we meet
perhaps setting a life on a different course—
one filled with excitement, adventure,
and sometimes even love.

Other Works by Karey White

Novels
My Own Mr. Darcy
For What It's Worth

Novella
Maggie's Song
(found in *A Timeless Romance Anthology: Love Letter Collection*)

For Veronica and Savannah,
My daughters and friends

One

ydia lifted her bag onto the scale and crossed her fingers it would meet the weight restrictions.

"Either you're a mighty fine packer or you're right lucky," said the man behind the counter. "Forty-nine pounds for one and forty-nine and a half pounds for this one." His thick, mahogany mustache moved as he spoke and reminded Lydia of a squirrel's tail.

"I guess I'm a little of both. I weighed them on a bathroom scale, but you never know how accurate they are. The scale said they'd be three pounds under."

"Now you know your scale weighs light. Probably didn't want to know that, did you?" He laughed at his little joke and Lydia tried not to stare at the rodent on his upper lip. "You need to go to Gate C-14. Glad you gave yourself some time. That gate's quite a jaunt from here."

Squirrel Man pointed to his right. "Go past the restaurants and stores, and you'll find the C concourse on your right. It's just past The Traveler's Friend. Now that's a piece'a irony, calling it a traveler's friend. I can buy a gallon of O.J. for what they're chargin' for a Dixie cup." He held his fingers up to demonstrate the tininess. Does that sound like a friend to you?"

Lydia laughed. "No, sir. It doesn't."

"You have a nice flight, Miss Sutton."

Lydia headed in the direction Squirrel Man had pointed. She'd taken only a few steps when the wheels of her carryon malfunctioned and the bag flipped onto its front side—the side without wheels—again. "This is the last trip I'm taking with you," she muttered to her suitcase. Of course, considering this summer, maybe she'd never take a trip again.

After Lydia made it through security, she stopped at a little deli and bought a sandwich before continuing to her gate. Squirrel Man had been right. The walk to C-14 was long, made even longer by the cheap wheels of her carryon.

Lydia felt clammy and uncomfortable. The air conditioning in North Carolina's humid heat was a ninety-pound weakling fighting a steroid-swollen heavyweight champion. The C concourse had to be at least the length of a football field. Up ahead was C-14—just past the mob of people waiting at C-12 for a flight to Miami.

Lydia maneuvered her way through the throng. "I'm so sorry," she said after her suitcase flopped over and upended an older gentleman's bag. Finally, the crowd thinned and she was at her gate, next to a few scattered early birds who sat in the powder-blue, vinyl chairs. Eyeing the seats facing the window, she cut through two rows. As she turned the corner, her suitcase flipped again and snagged on a chair leg, upsetting her balance. Her purse slipped down her arm to the crook of her elbow. Lydia wrenched the suitcase back to its wheels and kept moving. The purse, now dangling from her elbow, caught on the armrest of a chair, yanking her to a stop. Her Sensational Sandwich sack flew out of her hand and landed on the floor a few feet away.

Lydia took a deep, cleansing breath, unhooked the purse strap from the armrest, righted the carryon, and looked for her wayward sandwich.

"Is this what you're looking for?" asked a handsome man.

Perfect. Of course Lydia's sandwich acrobatics would have to be witnessed by a guy who looked like a movie star. And not a Nick-Nolte-mugshot movie star, either. This guy was more like a Ryan-Gosling-freshly-shaved-and-in-a-perfectly-tailored-navy-suit-with-a-super-crisp-white-shirt movie star.

"Thank you," she said and took her sandwich before dropping into the closest chair. Forget looking out the window. It wasn't worth the effort. Lydia blew the hair out of her eyes and dragged her bag closer to her feet.

"You doing okay?" the Ryan Gosling lookalike asked from across the aisle. Laughter was barely contained behind his very nice smile. Lydia sighed and shrugged her shoulders.

"I am now."

The man turned his attention back to his laptop, but his smile lasted several more seconds. Lydia pulled her turkey on wheat sandwich from the crumpled bag. She hadn't eaten since breakfast and that had been a sad little spread. Earlier in the week, Lydia had packed up Cambri's few remaining belongings and shipped them to Colorado. Yesterday, she had completely cleaned out the apartment, including the few condiments that were left in the refrigerator. She didn't want to lose her deposit because of a half bottle of ketchup and an expired jar of relish. This morning, the only thing left to eat had been a browning banana and the last few swallows of milk.

When Lydia took the second bite of her sandwich, a tablespoon-sized glob of mayonnaise oozed out the bottom and into her hand. She fumbled one-handed through the bag in search of a napkin. Was this a joke? The only thing left in the bag was a mayonnaise packet. Didn't need that. "I can watch your bag while you go wash up." It was the handsome man, and his mirth had reached beyond his fantastic smile (he had a perfect dimple that appeared by the right corner of his mouth) and up to his twinkling blue eyes. Lydia looked from the man to her fistful of mayonnaise. A robotic female voice in Lydia's mind recited lines about leaving bags unattended and not accepting packages from strangers. "I promise I won't take it and make a run for it," he said.

"You'd be terribly disappointed if you did," Lydia said, making up her mind. She returned the rest of her sandwich to the paper bag, pulled her purse onto her shoulder with her condimentless hand, and headed for the restroom, holding her mayonnaise like a gift in front of her. "I'll hurry."

When Lydia approached her seat a few minutes later, an airport security officer with a shiny face and a little paunch was standing in the aisle by her suitcase.

"Is this your bag?" he asked.

"Yes. Is everything okay?" Why hadn't she paid attention to the voice in her head?

"It appeared to be left unattended. In the future, I'd advise you to either take your bag with you or move it closer to your boyfriend when you leave."

Lydia shot a surprised glance at the movie star, and he shrugged. "Sorry, babe. I told him you'd be right back, and I offered to move your bag over by me, but he wanted me to wait for you to come back."

Lydia almost choked. She knew he was just rescuing her from the security guard, but no one had ever, ever called Lydia "babe" before and certainly no one as handsome as Ryan Gosling. It had a wonderful ring to it. Was her racing heart because of being questioned by an officer of the law or because this man had just called her "babe?"

Lydia dragged her distracted gaze back to the much less interesting man standing by her bag. "I'm so sorry. I just had to make a little run to the ladies' room. It won't happen again."

"See that it doesn't. Airport security is no laughing matter." Was she laughing? "Have a nice flight."

Lydia sat down by her bag. "You should probably move over here by me since you're my girlfriend. We don't want to make him suspicious."

"Oh. Of course. I should have thought of that." Did the movie star want Lydia to sit by him? Lydia rolled her eyes at her silliness. He was just trying to keep from being hassled any further. He went back to working on his laptop as she moved her things across the aisle. "Sorry about that," Lydia whispered.

"No problem." He looked up from his computer and smiled. Oh. My. Wow! Up close his dimple was even cuter. The bigger the smile, the deeper the dimple. "Are you taking a trip to Denver?" he asked.

"What?" She dragged her eyes away from his mouth. "Oh. I'm headed home."

"You're *from* Denver?"

"Just north. I live in Bridger."

"I live in downtown Denver," he said. "I'm Blake, by the way."

"I'm Lydia."

"What brought you to North Carolina?"

Lydia shook her head and sighed. Telling the truth about her summer in Charlotte was humiliating and disappointing. Of course, she could make something up, but that was the cowardly thing to do and this summer was supposed to have been about being brave and adventurous.

"You can't say?" he asked when she didn't answer. "Was it some top secret mission you can't talk about?" He sat up a little straighter and closed his laptop.

Lydia tried not to stare at his mischievous eyes as she thought about how to answer. A little piece of bravery with this stranger wouldn't salvage her failed summer, but at least she could finish with a tiny victory. She took a deep breath. "I was supposed to have a summer full of adventure and new experiences, but unfortunately, I learned I'm not very adventurous." Blake looked confused, so Lydia explained. "My friend loaned me her condo for the summer. Her instructions were to 'go somewhere new every day. Meet new people. Do adventurous things.' I'm afraid I failed."

"Come on, I'm sure you did *something* adventurous," Blake said.

Lydia shook her head. "Nothing." She reached down and unzipped the pocket of her suitcase. "Unless you call sitting on a lounge chair on the roof of the condo with a book an adventure." She pulled out three books and held them up one at a time. "Look at these. *Quest for Parts Unknown* is about this guy searching for the remains of an expedition to the North Pole forty years ago. They never returned, so he was trying to discover what happened to them. He got caught in a terrible storm and barely made it back alive. *From Sea to Shining Sea.* This woman lost her job and broke up with her boyfriend, so she decided since she had nothing tying her down, she'd walk from the tip of Florida to the top corner of Washington, relying only on the kindness of strangers. It took her almost five months, but she did it."

Lydia started to hold up up the third book then blushed. "I read about other people's adventures," she said as she moved to tuck the books back into her bag, "but I didn't have any of my own."

"Come on. I don't get to see that last book?" Blake asked.

Lydia was caught. Without looking at him, she handed Blake the book. The cover was embarrassing. A male model with perfectly floppy hair had his hands over the eyes of a female model in a "Guess who?" kind of pose. It was brightly backlit and the title was written in a romantic, flowing script. The woman at the bookstore had gushed about it and Lydia hadn't wanted to hurt her feelings, so ten minutes and $12 later, it left the store in Lydia's bag. "*Love at Tenth Sight?*

What's this one about?" Blake didn't even try to stifle his laugh, and Lydia's blush deepened.

"It's about a woman who's given up on love because she's had her heart broken so many times and, finally, she meets her soul mate."

"Had she actually had her heart broken nine times?"

Lydia wished she'd left that book in her bag."Well, I haven't finished it, but yeah, I guess so."

"You spent your summer reading these?"

"These and about a dozen others," Lydia admitted.

Blake whistled. "Sounds relaxing, but you're right. Not very adventurous."

Lydia shoved the books in her bag. "I wasted an entire summer, and now I get to go back and report that I'm dull and unadventurous."

"You have to give a report?"

"That was the deal. Free condo in exchange for a full report of my summer exploits."

Lydia wanted to kick herself. This had been a once in a lifetime chance to do whatever she wanted. School was out, so she'd had no students to look after and no principal to report to. With Jace and Cambri checking in on Grandpa, nothing had stood between Lydia and three months of excitement.

On her first day in town, she'd stopped at a trendy hotel and picked up brochures about kite-surfing and a bike tour through civil war battlegrounds. She'd thought about backpacking into Great Smoky Mountains National Park and camping overnight by herself. That would have been adventurous and even a little rebellious because she knew her mother would totally disapprove. Lydia had even scouted out a singles mix-and-mingle at a local bookstore and speed dating at a nice restaurant not far from the condo.

But Lydia hadn't done any of it.

"I did try Indian food," she said, shaking her head. "I wanted to have something exciting to tell my students when we did the 'what did you do this summer' assignment so they'd think I was a cool teacher. Somehow, I don't think they'll be impressed that I ate curry."

"You teach school?"

"I teach fifth grade at Juniper Heights Elementary. It's in Fort Collins." Blake's face looked sympathetic, and Lydia hated how pitiful she sounded.

"Don't feel too bad," Blake said. "I'm headed home as a failure, too." Lydia lifted an eyebrow. "I just wasted three days I couldn't afford to lose on a wild goose chase. Now I'm headed home with nothing to show for it."

"What kind of goose chase?" Lydia asked. "Unless you can't tell me because it's classified."

Blake showed his dimple. "My grandfather made me promise I'd go find a woman named Gladys. She's had a box of his things for more than fifty years, and I was supposed to get it."

"More than fifty years?" Lydia asked. "She probably doesn't even have it anymore."

"That's what I thought. But Grandpa called her last year, and she still has it. He told her he had a grandson who needed to see what was in the box, and she said to send him to North Carolina for it. Except I can't find her. She doesn't live at the address he gave me, and the woman that lives there now has no idea where she is."

"Why do you need to see it?"

"I don't know. He said when I saw it, I'd understand."

"So you're leaving with nothing?"

"Oh no, I've got something. I've got $800 in wasted air fare and a stack of paperwork even deeper than when I left."

"I'm sorry," Lydia said.

"It wouldn't be a big deal, but I'm so close to making partner, and I don't want anyone to think I've lost my focus."

"Partner where?"

"Collins, Strider and Van Wagoner."

"I'm sure you'll be fine. Just tell them you worked while you were away," Lydia said, pointing at his laptop.

"And you can tell your friend you ate Indian food." They laughed.

Blake put his laptop in his briefcase while he spoke. "The worst part is that I was really curious about what Grandpa wanted me to have."

"Can't he just tell you what it was?"

Blake shook his head. "He died in April." He leaned forward, his elbows on his knees, fingers clasped in front of him, and stared absently across the wide concourse.

"I'm sorry." Instinctively, Lydia put her hand on his arm. Horrified, she snatched it back. What was she doing touching this man? He was a handsome stranger, and she was an unadventurous schoolteacher whose only human interactions over the past three months had been with the clerk at the bookstore and the takeout deliverymen. She had no business touching him.

Blake turned his head toward her and smiled. Lydia felt short of breath and hoped he couldn't tell that her jackhammer heart was trying to demolish her ribs and escape her chest.

"Thanks, Lydia. I should have come as soon as he told me about it, but things at the office were busy and I didn't want to look like I was making something more important than the firm. I guess I figured I had time."

"Will you try to find her another time?"

"I don't know. I have a letter he wanted me to read after I'd gone through everything in the box. That might tell me something, but it feels wrong to read it without doing what he asked. It's like I'm cheating him."

"Attention passengers."

The voice sounded like Mrs. Jackson, Lydia's sophomore history teacher. Mrs. Jackson had recited the same test questions for forty years and sounded like a recording that had been slowed down to half speed. "Who

9

was an American mechanical engineer who used scientific management to improve industrial efficiency in the early twentieth century?" By the time she'd read the question, the class was nearly asleep.

"Flight 1758 from Charlotte to Denver has been delayed by thirty minutes. Again, flight one seven five eight from Charlotte to Denver has been delayed by thirty minutes. We apologize for any inconvenience. Please see the counter if you have any questions or if you have connecting flights in Denver. Thank you."

Blake and Lydia looked at each other and laughed. "Wow. Glad she got that out before the thirty minute delay was over," Blake said. "I guess I have time to go get myself a sandwich."

"I'll watch your bags," Lydia said with a smile. She was surprised when Blake slid his briefcase and duffle bag a little closer to her feet.

"I should probably tell them to go light on the mayo, right?" he said.

"Good idea. And be sure they give you some napkins."

Instinctively, Lydia started to pull out her book, but not wanting to be caught reading *Love at Tenth Sight* when Blake returned, she changed her mind and watched two children playing Uno on the floor.

"I hope you like brownies," Blake said when he returned ten minutes later.

"I love brownies."

"Good. I was afraid you might tell me you were allergic to chocolate."

"Sometimes I wish that were true. Thank you. That was thoughtful of you."

Blake ate his sandwich, and Lydia took a bite of the brownie. "Mmm. This is good. Would you like some of it?"

"Thanks. I've got one for myself in the bag," he said.

"Attention passengers." Thankfully it was a new voice, and this one spoke at a normal speed.

"Uh oh," Blake said.

"Due to mechanical difficulties, flight 1758 from Charlotte to Denver has been cancelled. Please bring your tickets to the counter to reschedule. Again, flight One Seven Five Eight, from Charlotte to Denver, has been cancelled. Please bring your tickets to the counter to reschedule your flight."

The world came alive around them. Snatches of conversations could be heard as people gathered their belongings.

"They'd better be giving us a free flight for this."

"And how about some food vouchers. I'm starving."

"I'd rather they cancel the flight than send us off in a faulty airplane."

"I'm going to miss my connecting flight."

"Well, that's not very convenient," Lydia said. "At least I have something to read."

Blake laughed. "I think they have to make arrangements for us to get on a flight right away, even if it's with another airline."

Blake and Lydia stayed in their seats as the area around them cleared and a line formed. Finally, Blake stood, picked up his duffel bag and briefcase, then waited while Lydia gathered her things. They took a spot at the back of the line. After a minute, Lydia spoke.

"Since you have to change your flight anyway, maybe you should stay another day or two and try to find the box."

The corner of Blake's mouth twitched. "Maybe you should stay a couple of days and have an adventure."

"Touché. I guess if the plane had gone down, I'd have had an adventure to tell about. Or not tell about."

The line moved slowly. "You know," Blake said. "Maybe your adventure could be staying and helping me find my grandfather's box."

Lydia nearly choked on her last bite of brownie. Was he joking? They didn't even know each other.

"I have to be back for teacher's meetings. And I need to get my classroom ready for school to start. The desks are all stacked up in a corner of the room and I need to get them set up and organized and I've got to put up a couple of bulletin boards. And I have to get papers for the parents copied for back to school night and…" Blake's smile widened as she spoke. "And I'm babbling, aren't I?"

"Yeah. Don't worry about it. I should get back to the office anyway. It was a crazy idea."

"Yeah," Lydia said, relieved. A few minutes passed, and they neared the front of the line. A voice in Lydia's head wouldn't be quiet. *You're a coward. You don't really want an adventure. You're all talk. You could kill two birds with one stone. Have an adventure and help this guy find the box from his grandfather. But you're too big of a wimp.* She wanted to tell the voice to mind its own business, but it wouldn't shut up. *Chicken. Scaredy cat. But this wasn't about adventure. This was about good, common sense, right? It wouldn't be smart to stay with this man she didn't know.* And yet her instincts told her this guy was safe, that she didn't need to fear his intentions.

It seemed the only way to stop the nag in her head was to speak. "It wasn't a crazy idea. It was an adventurous idea. And I came here for adventure. I need something to tell Cambri when I get home, right? And you need to find that box or you'll miss out on something important. And I don't technically have to be back until Wednesday morning, so…"

"Really? Are you just talking a big game?" Blake teased.

"You're not a psychopathic killer, are you?"

"No. But I certainly wouldn't tell you if I was."

"That's true. That would really up the whole adventure factor, though."

"See, you're braver than you thought."

"Do you really want to do this?" Lydia asked, not sure what she wanted his answer to be.

"I don't know if I'll make it back here any time soon, and it would be nice to feel like I gave it an extra effort."

"Maybe this cancelled flight is a sign. But I really do have to be at work Wednesday morning."

"So do I. If we fly home Tuesday, that gives us two days to find Gladys."

"Oh help," Lydia whispered, and Blake laughed, showing his dimple. That was all it took. When they reached the front of the line, Blake and Lydia changed their flights to the 8:10 departing flight on Tuesday evening.

Two

hat was he thinking? Blake didn't have time for this. He'd been worried about work the entire time he'd been in North Carolina and now, on a whim, he'd nearly doubled the length of his trip.

Blake stood a little behind Lydia at the luggage carousel waiting for the bags she'd checked two hours earlier. He'd managed his short trip with only his duffle and briefcase, but Lydia had just spent three months in North Carolina. That, of course, required extra bags.

"There are two of them, and I tied a yellow polka-dot ribbon to the handles, so they'll be easy to identify," Lydia said over her shoulder.

Of course she had. She looked like a girl who'd have a drawer of crafty ribbons and construction paper. She probably crocheted booties for her friends' new babies and delivered elaborately decorated cupcakes to new neighbors.

Blake fired off an email to his assistant, Brynn, telling her of his change of plans. He cringed as he thought of Brynn relaying the message to Pryce. Of course, Pryce would be unhappy with this development and would probably call

Blake tomorrow to let him know exactly how this would impact his future.

Pryce Van Wagoner. Just three weeks ago, he'd sat across the chrome and glass desk that probably cost more than a year's rent for Blake's one bedroom apartment. Mr. Van Wagoner had looked dark and forbidding against the wall of windows that boasted a view of Denver's business district. "You're doing good work here, Blake."

"Thank you, Mr. Van Wagoner."

"You can call me Pryce."

Blake nodded and wiped his sweaty palms on his trousers. "I keep hearing your name. Phoebe and Brian are calling you a star, and Don says you're going to end up being our youngest partner."

"I appreciate that, sir. It's definitely what I'm working toward."

"I looked over your files for the Challis-Austin merger, and I'm very pleased. If this deal closes according to plan, it would be difficult for us to ignore you when we start the selection process."

"And it should go well, sir. It's on track, and I see no reason why it shouldn't close by the middle of September. We all want to have everything in place before the final quarter."

"Good to hear." Pryce had stepped around the desk and shaken Blake's hand, adding a partnerly slap on the back. "Keep up the good work. I'm eager to watch you wrap up this deal."

The luggage carousel started spitting out bags, and Blake took a step closer. He should have booked a seat on the next flight home. For two years, he'd put work before everything else. He'd missed family events. He hadn't done anything with friends for months, and dating the past two years had been almost nonexistent. He couldn't believe he'd just put his job on the back burner so he could traipse around North Carolina with a girl he didn't know.

Of course he wanted to find his grandfather's box, but Blake knew that wasn't the only reason he'd jumped at this arrangement, and it baffled him. Sure, Lydia was cute, but she wasn't the type of girl who turned every head in the room. She certainly wasn't the kind of girl who would inspire a man to rearrange his career goals. But wasn't that what he'd just done?

He looked at her closely. Lydia was very girl next door—blonde, blue-eyed and… what? Natural. She wore almost no makeup, her hair smelled like fruity shampoo, and there was a light in her eyes. Although Blake hadn't dated much in the past two years, his former girlfriends had been more polished and put-together. They'd have marked their luggage with a chrome tag, not a polka-dot ribbon. Blake's reaction to Lydia was surprising and even frustrating. He couldn't be thinking about a cute girl who blushed easily when he needed to be concentrating on the upcoming merger.

Lydia glanced his way, and when she saw him looking at her, she smiled and blushed. She really was adorable. He forced his eyes back to the luggage carousel, and his mind to think about his job.

The Challis-Austin merger was a tricky one. Both sides wanted it to happen—Mary Challis needed it to happen—but they each wanted to feel like they were getting the best end of the deal. It would already have wrapped up if they hadn't been dancing around the middle ground for weeks, tweaking the terms and adding stipulations. They were still on track for a mid-September close, but Blake didn't like being so far away at this crucial time.

Why had Grandpa been so demanding? He'd known Blake's goal and how hard he'd have to work to reach it. Grandpa had been a successful man. He'd climbed the ranks at Denver General from brand new doctor to Hospital Chief of Staff. He knew why Blake was so focused, and yet he'd insisted Blake hunt down some relic from the past. *Stubborn old man.*

As soon as that thought entered his mind, Blake was filled with guilt. Grandpa had loved him. Blake knew that. If Grandpa wanted him to retrieve this box, he must have felt it was important, so even though the timing stunk, Blake would do his best to find it.

And he'd do his best not to be distracted by Lydia or the smell of her hair. Or her cute clumsiness. Or the way her hand had felt on his arm.

Still, the timing could have been better.

"There's one," Lydia said and reached for the first bag with the bright ribbon.

"I'll get it," Blake said. He lifted the suitcase off the carousel and put it with their other bags. A few seconds later, another ribboned bag popped over the lip of the conveyor belt and slid with a thud to the wall. Blake lifted it off and extended the handle, pulling it along beside him.

"Should we make a plan?" Lydia asked. She sounded a little nervous, and Blake wondered if she regretted this act of spontaneity.

"We know we need a car, so let's do that first."

"Sounds like a plan," Lydia said with a smile. Oh boy, she was cute. Blake was in trouble.

They rented a midsize sedan and left the airport behind them. Over an early dinner at a teal and chrome diner, they made a more formal plan.

"I went to the address my Grandpa had for Gladys," Blake said, "but there was a young family living there. They bought the house six months ago, and they didn't know Gladys. A lot can happen in a year."

She drew her brows together as she took a drink of lemonade. "Did you check with the neighbors?"

"I knocked on the houses next door, but no one was home."

"Sounds like we'd better go canvas the street she lived on."

Blake smiled. "Canvas the street? You said you're a teacher, right?"

"I teach fifth grade. And I've read every Nancy Drew and Hardy Boys book there is. Hurry and finish your fries, and let's start sleuthing."

They drove to a quiet neighborhood on the outskirts of Charlotte. Belmont Street was straight out of a Norman Rockwell painting. Trees lined the streets, their old, thick roots having their way with the sidewalks. The houses were small bungalows, built by sensible people who'd just survived the depression, nothing like the excessive houses in the suburbs with their equally bloated mortgages.

"That's the one she lived in," Blake said, pointing at a small yellow house with a tricycle in the front yard. "I knocked on both of those houses, but no one was home."

They knocked again on the white house next door. A pimply teenage boy with no shirt answered the door.

"Sorry, man," he said after Blake asked about Gladys. "I noticed she was gone, but I have no idea where she went."

"Do you think your parents would know?" Lydia asked.

"There's just my dad, but he's at work. He's working a double so he won't be home until early tomorrow morning."

They thanked him and walked to the gray house on the other side. The sidewalk to the door was lined with rose bushes. A chorus of yapping dogs answered their knock, but no one came to the door.

"Excuse me," said a young woman from the front yard of the home that had belonged to Gladys. She held a diaper-clad baby. "Are you the one who was looking for Gladys Baker?"

"I am," Blake said as he and Lydia walked back to meet her in the narrow driveway.

"After you left, I was talking to Beulah Edwards. She lives in that house right there." She pointed at a brick house across the street and near the corner. "She said that she and

Gladys knew each other and if you came back to send you her way."

"Thank you," Blake said and shook her hand. "I really appreciate it."

"No problem. Good luck."

Beulah's doorbell was chimes playing "God Rest Ye Merry Gentlemen" slightly off key, which didn't fit with the sweltering heat and humidity of the August afternoon. "Maybe no one's home," Blake said after they'd waited more than a minute.

"I thought I heard something." Lydia knocked and they waited a little longer.

Finally, an elderly woman opened the door and looked at them through the screen. "I hope you're not selling anything." She lifted her thick glasses from her eyes to her forehead and looked back and forth between Blake and Lydia. "See. It says no soliciting right there." She pointed her elbow at a handwritten sign taped below the doorbell.

"We're not selling anything," Lydia said. "Are you Beulah?"

"I was last time I checked," she said and chuckled at her joke.

Lydia smiled. "My name is Lydia, and this is Blake. We're looking for Gladys Baker, and your neighbor said you might know where she lives now."

"Of course I do. Gladys was my dear friend. We used to go walking together almost every day. How do you know her?"

"She and my grandfather were friends many years ago," Blake said.

"Hmm. Well, come on in, and I'll get you her address." She pushed the screen door open. Blake held it for Lydia. After the bright, afternoon sun, it took a moment for their eyes to adjust to the darkness of the house. The air was hot and stuffy. A muted television sat in the living room, an old episode of *Jeopardy* on the screen. "Go on now. Sit down," Beulah said from the kitchen. "I've got the address in here somewhere. No need to stand there while I hunt it down."

Blake and Lydia sat on the edge of a maroon floral sofa with doilies covering the arms. The room smelled faintly of burnt toast and Icy Hot. A cat appeared from under the couch and rubbed against Blake's legs, circling his ankles over and over. He moved his legs, and the cat matched his moves, arching its back as it marked Blake as its territory.

"I think it likes you," Lydia whispered and giggled.

In the kitchen, Beulah rummaged through drawers and cupboards, muttering to herself. *Jeopardy* went to a commercial and came back to the Double Jeopardy round, but still Beulah didn't return. Blake scooted the cat away with his hand, but a minute later it was back. Alex Trebek was reading the last column of answers when Beulah finally shuffled into the room waving a piece of paper.

"I knew I had it in there." She glanced at the television. "Blue blazes, what's that hippy doin' fixin' to win? He doesn't look smart enough to beat those others. That man in the middle is a college professor and that woman's a lawyer. They shouldn't be lettin' some upstart beat them." She turned back toward her guests on the sofa. "They oughta have a dress code or something on these shows, make people clean up and cut their hair or they can't come on and play."

Blake nodded, glad that his hair had been recently trimmed, and Lydia bit the sides of her mouth to keep from laughing. Beulah stood in front of her chair until the show went to a commercial then she carefully lowered herself into her rocking recliner. "You can bring Sajak to me if you don't want him loving your leg," she said.

Blake picked up the cat and handed him to Beulah. Sajak turned a circle on her lap before he snuggled in. "I knew I had this in there, I just couldn't find it. I thought I put it in my little address book, but it wasn't there, so I looked through the junk drawer and the bills on my table. Wouldn't you know, I was right in the first place? It was in my little address book, but I stuck the darn thing under G for Gladys instead of B for Baker. I s'pose I shoulda put it both places so an old bat like me could track it down. I'm not even sure why I asked Francie for it. Francie is Gladys's granddaughter. It's not like I can drive out to see her. They took my license away two years ago 'cause I parked on the sidewalk. I swear they made the sidewalks down on Clemway so wide, I thought it was the road. A sidewalk should look like a sidewalk, not like a four-lane. Okay, be still. It's Final Jeopardy." She unmuted the television and Alex gave the final answer. "Come on now, Professor," Beulah said as the music played and the contestants wrote their answers. "You can beat him."

"Ah burnt grits and gravy," Beulah said and punched the mute button on her remote as Alex shook hands with the long-haired winner. "What did y'all need?" she asked looking at Blake and Lydia again.

"We're trying to find Gladys Baker," Blake said.

"Oh, right. Here it is. Gladys fell and bumped her head last winter. After that, she got all confused and forgot to get dressed in the morning, so Francie had her moved to a home where they'd remind her to eat and put her clothes on. It wasn't a nursing home. Francie wouldn'ta put her in a nursing home. It was one of those nice places where they have social activities and fix ya dinner and you have your own little apartment. Gladys even got to take some of her own furniture. She said it was a real nice place, just like the name." She held up the paper. "Shady Days Manor. Doesn't that sound just lovely? It's over in Hickory. You can write down the address and phone number if you like."

Lydia took the paper and entered the information into her phone.

Beulah shook her head. "You kids have phones like a typewriter. Don't even need pencils and paper anymore."

"Thank you, Beulah. You've been very helpful," Blake said and they each shook her hand. Blake held up his hand when Beulah started to pull herself out of the chair. "We can let ourselves out."

"Yes, that would be good. I'll just stay here and watch *Wheel of Fortune* with Sajak."

Back in the car, Blake turned to Lydia. "I guess we should think about where to stay tonight."

"I wish I still had a key to Cambri's condo. I could have stayed there."

"Let's get a couple of rooms at that Residence Inn we passed out by the airport. They have laundry there. I've either got to wash clothes or go shopping, and I'd much rather wash clothes."

Three

They booked two rooms for the next two nights, and after a mildly awkward goodnight in the hall, Lydia and Blake parted ways. Blake's room was next door to Lydia's, and after a while, she heard him leave. Probably to go wash his clothes. She wished she'd offered to keep him company. If only she were brave enough to do that, she thought with annoyance.

Today had probably been the bravest day of Lydia's life. She'd pretended Blake was her boyfriend to get rid of a security guard. She'd suggested he stay and search for his grandfather's box then agreed to stay with him. She'd spent the afternoon and evening with a man she'd only just met and was planning to spend the next two days with him. So she hadn't gone with him to the laundry room. Big deal. She'd been courageous today and she would give herself credit for that.

Was this adventurous enough to make up for her summer of seclusion? Probably not. But Lydia still felt proud of herself.

She was flipping through the channels of the muted television when her phone rang. As she fished it out of her purse, she hoped it was Blake, but then realized they hadn't exchanged numbers. This made her feel strangely uneasy. She'd call his room when he got back and ask for his number.

Her phone quit ringing before she found it. The screen showed a missed call from her mother, and Lydia felt a wave of panic.

Lydia's parents had moved to Arizona, but that didn't stop Mom from calling regularly and keeping tabs on her little girl. She knew as much about Lydia's life now as she had when they'd been living in the same house. Mom would certainly not approve of this little arrangement, even with the separate rooms.

Lydia was tempted not to call her mother back, but she couldn't leave her hanging for two more days. Mom would start to worry, and soon she and Dad would be arranging a search party. Might as well get it over with.

"Lydia," her mom said into the phone after one ring. "I just tried to call you."

Lydia laughed. "I know. That's why I'm calling you back."

"Oh, of course." Her mom laughed with her. "I was just checking in to make sure you got home okay."

"Actually, I'm not home yet. I'm still in Charlotte."

"Weren't you going home today?"

"I was. Our flight got cancelled for mechanical difficulties, and when I rescheduled the flight, I got a ticket for Tuesday night."

"I thought you had to be back at school tomorrow." Her mom sounded concerned.

"I was planning to be so I could get my room ready, but I'll just have to do that after the teacher's meetings on Wednesday. It'll be fine."

"It seems like they ought to have been able to get you home sooner than two days. You should file a complaint."

"I could have gotten on a flight tonight, but I decided to stay."

"You must be having fun. Are you staying in Cambri's condo?"

"I turned the keys to the condo in this morning. We're staying at a Residence Inn."

"We?" Lydia couldn't believe she'd just slipped like that. She didn't want to mislead her mom, but she didn't want her worrying either. She'd spend the next two days and nights imagining every terrifying scene from *Taken*.

"Yes, Mom. I wasn't the only one on the cancelled flight."

Mom laughed. "Right. Of course. Well, honey, lock your door. And not just the regular lock. Be sure to use the dead bolt and put that bar across the door. And don't answer it for anyone. Does the door have a peephole?"

Lydia scooted to the end of the bed so she could see the door. "Yes, it does. And I'm already locked up tight. No need to worry. Listen, Mom, I'm really tired. I was just getting ready for bed."

"All right, Liddie Lou. I love you, honey."

"I love you, too, Mom," Lydia said. "I'll let you know when I get home."

Lydia felt terrible as she got ready for bed. The only time she'd purposely misled her mother was when she and Jace had planned a surprise birthday party for Mom's fortieth birthday.

Lydia watched a home makeover show with the sound off so she could hear Blake return to his room, but her eyelids felt so heavy.

Just before seven the next morning, her room phone rang, startling Lydia awake with its brash, early morning sound. Some people with ridiculously toned and tanned bodies were dancing and sweating on the silent television screen. Sunshine seeped in from around the drawn drapes.

She fumbled for the phone. "Hello."

"Hey, Lydia. Did I wake you up?" It was Blake. She must have fallen asleep before he came back to his room.

"Yeah, actually you did."

"Sorry. I thought we could go down to breakfast together."

"That'd be great."

"I'm just getting into the shower. Can you be ready in forty-five minutes? I'd like to try to leave the hotel by eight-thirty."

"Definitely. Just knock on my door."

Lydia showered and put on a pale green belted peasant dress. She shook out her hands to help calm herself when she realized how nervous she was to see Blake. *Settle down. It's not like this is a date or anything.*

"You look great," Blake said when they were in the elevator.

"Thanks." He looked great, too. He was wearing a pair of navy chinos rolled up at the hem with a gray polo shirt.

"But maybe you should change into some shorts or jeans," he said. Lydia looked at him curiously. He was staring nonchalantly at the door of the elevator.

"You really think I need to change?"

A smile cracked Blake's casual demeanor. "Okay, fine. I've got a little surprise and a dress won't really work."

"What kind of surprise?" Lydia met his playful smile with one of her own.

"You know I'm not going to tell you. Just change after we eat. You'll be glad you did."

"Aren't we going to Shady Days today?"

"We sure are. Right after we make a pit stop."

Lydia's mind was preoccupied at breakfast. She wanted to exchange cell phone numbers, but she was nervous to suggest it. What if he thought she was forward? This was ridiculous. This was why she'd sat paralyzed in Cambri's apartment for three months. She thought and thought about every move until she'd either missed the opportunity or talked herself out of it. She wanted to have his number. She wanted him to have hers. *So be brave and ask for it, for heaven's sake.*

"Hey Blake, I was thinking last night that we should probably give each other our cell numbers. I mean, my bag is in your car, and we're flying home together tomorrow. We should probably have some way of reaching each other. You know, we might need to call each other for something or we might get separated or—"

"Lydia," Blake said, and his mouth quirked like his dimple couldn't decide if it wanted to make an appearance or not. "Put your number in my phone." He gave her his phone. "And hand me yours."

Blake acted like it was no big deal. Why did she always have to make things so hard?

After breakfast, Lydia changed into a pair of jean capris and a pink and white striped t-shirt. It was hard to keep her excitement in check. What kind of surprise could he have planned? Better not get her hopes up. He probably thought a stop at the bookstore would be an exciting surprise for her. He'd be right. But why the pants?

"We needed to get on that onramp," Lydia said in the car, as they passed the road they needed.

"I know. We'll head that way soon."

"Should I be nervous? Are you kidnapping me?" Lydia asked.

"Yes, I'm kidnapping you. And yeah, you should probably be a little nervous. I know I am."

If his voice hadn't held a note of teasing, Lydia might have panicked, but his excitement filled the car with a new energy, and Lydia's heart started thumping a little harder. Blake must have seen her twisting her fingers together nervously because he reached over and patted her hand. "Don't worry. It'll be fun." He put his hand back on the steering wheel. Suddenly, Lydia could think of nothing except his hand on hers.

Blake's phone rang, and he answered it. "Hi, Brynn. You must have gotten my email." He waited for her response. "I know. The timing isn't good. But my flight was cancelled, and I needed a couple more days to track down this inheritance." Pause. "I know. I was hoping you could call Mary Challis's assistant—her name is Jean Crawley—and get their final numbers. After we have all those, we can email it to both of them for their approval. When those come back, we'll be ready to put together the final documents."

Lydia could hear Brynn's voice, but she couldn't make out the words. "I'm sorry. It's only two more days. Please just take care of that for me. I'll owe you big." Blake's face had gone from happy and playful to drawn and worried in just a couple of minutes. "I'm pulling over right now, and I'll get the number for you."

"Sorry," Blake mouthed as he pulled into a parking lot.

"It's okay," Lydia whispered back.

Blake pulled his briefcase from the back seat and gave Brynn a name and phone number. "Don't worry. I'll be back in the office on Wednesday morning and you can call me if you need to." He listened to Brynn talk while he put the briefcase back. "I have a pretty good lead today. I'm going to see her at an assisted living facility. Call me if you need anything else. And thanks, Brynn."

Blake hit the off button on his phone and let out a long sigh. He leaned his head against the back of his seat and massaged the bridge of his nose.

"Is everything okay?" Lydia asked.

"Sure. I just have some big things going on at work."

"Maybe I shouldn't have suggested this."

Blake looked at her concerned face. "I'm glad you did. I really should get this box, and it's better that I do it now instead of having to make another trip. Besides, if I'd done it later, I'd have been doing it on my own instead of with your help." He smiled. "I'd rather do it with you."

This wasn't good. All Blake had to do was smile and Lydia could hardly breathe, which meant she'd probably make a fool of herself. She'd stumble over her words or she'd blush constantly instead of just occasionally. Or maybe she'd do something embarrassing, like spill food on herself or split her pants.

"I guess we'd better get busy then. I'd hate for you to get behind at work and have nothing to show for it. Maybe we should skip this little surprise detour and just head to Hickory."

"No way. We'll get to Hickory soon enough. We're doing this."

Blake put the car in gear, and ten minutes later, they pulled into a small, private hangar not far from the airport.

"What's going on, Blake?" Lydia asked. Her stomach was already in knots, and she wasn't even sure what they were doing.

"We're going skydiving."

Lydia shook her head. "No we're not."

"Yes, we are."

"No. We're really not." Lydia's voice cracked.

"Are you pregnant?"

"No," Lydia said indignantly.

"Do you have a heart condition?"

"No, but I think I might if you don't turn around."

Blake pulled the car up to a long, flat building painted bright orange. The sign said, "Charlotte Skydiving: The best way to see Charlotte is from the sky." He put the car in park and turned in his seat to face her. "Listen, Lydia. You're helping me. I'm going to help you. This will give you something to report to your friend, and once you do this, your fifth graders will think you're the coolest teacher ever."

Lydia tore her eyes away from Blake's face and looked at the garish building in front of her. That bright orange was probably supposed to look fun, but right now it was just hurting her eyes. She took several shaky breaths. She knew

Blake was right. This could help her salvage her unadventurous summer. If she lived through it. "Are you doing it too?" she asked.

"If you don't mind sharing the fun."

Lydia shook her head. "No. I mean, yes. I mean, no, I don't mind sharing and yes, I want you to do it with me."

"Then let's go."

Four

L ast night, as he'd waited for his clothes to dry, Blake had searched the internet, looking for adventurous activities they could fit into the next forty-eight hours. He'd found several lists of suggestions. Some were out of the question—cage diving with alligators in Australia and racing water buffalo in Indonesia. Biking the Pacific Coast Highway was logistically impossible, and somehow Blake didn't think Lydia would enjoy rolling and smoking her own cigars.

But he'd found a couple of things that were possibilities, and this was one of them. Blake had never been skydiving, but the website had made it sound fun. After reading a few customer reviews and the qualifications of the professionals who'd be jumping with them, he'd selected Charlotte Skydiving. The biggest draw was that they could jump one right after the other, so they could experience it together. One pair said they were so close in the air, they could see each other's expressions. Something about watching Lydia's face as they plummeted through the sky was very appealing to him. He'd called before breakfast and scheduled the jump.

Buster and Liam were their instructors and would be jumping with them. Liam was short, muscular and so tanned you could practically see cancer cells multiplying. Buster had a bushy blond beard and a ponytail. When Buster explained what to do in the unlikely event that the chute didn't open, Blake began to wonder if he'd made a mistake. Lydia looked like the Cullen clan had sucked her dry, and she was biting her bottom lip so hard, he feared she might bite through it. She clasped her hands together in a tight little ball on her lap, and her feet were hooked around the legs of her chair.

"Any questions?" Buster asked. When neither of them answered, he said, "All right. Come with us, and we'll get you suited up."

Blake stood, but Lydia seemed stuck to her chair. "Are you okay?" he asked her. Lydia's head gave an indecisive roll. Was that a nod yes or a shake no? It was probably a little of both. Blake reached down to help her up. Her hand was freezing. She unwound her legs from the chair and let him pull her to her feet, but when he started to let go, she grasped his hand tightly.

"This will be fun," he said. When she didn't answer, he stopped in the hall. "Hey, if you really don't want to do this, you don't have to. I'm not going to force it on you." The truth was, Blake would have been fine backing out. This wasn't something he needed to do to die happy.

Lydia took a deep breath. Her voice came out, but just barely. "I really want to do it. I'm just terrified."

Blake tamped down the nerves he'd been feeling. He wanted to help her do this, and if it meant putting on a brave face, he would. "I read last night that they have to jump more than two hundred times before they're allowed to jump tandem with someone. They know what they're doing. Let's just have fun." Lydia nodded but didn't let go of his hand. Blake didn't mind.

"Thought we lost you," Buster said when they walked into the room where they'd dress. Dozens of flight suits hung according to size against one wall. On another wall were parachute packs and goggles. Lydia pulled her hair back into a tight bun then Liam helped her get into her suit while Buster helped Blake. Liam was flirty and talkative, and Blake was glad to see Lydia laugh.

"I can't believe I'm doing this," Lydia said as they stepped out of the building.

"After you do it once, you'll want to do it a thousand times," Buster said.

Across the tarmac was a small plane. Blake had never been in a plane this small, and his stomach tightened.

"You're about to have your adventure," he said.

"Thanks to you. And let's not get ahead of ourselves. I haven't jumped yet."

Instead of seats, the plane was equipped with a long bench that led up to the door. Blake sat in front of Buster. Ahead of him were Liam and Lydia. Blake would have felt awkward wedged tightly between the two instructors, except that his mind was too occupied with what was coming.

The engine roared to life, and it was hard to hear anything else. They taxied down the runway and soon they were flying higher and higher above the green, North Carolina countryside. Liam was yelling last-minute instructions to Lydia, who nodded, put her goggles in place, and grasped her shoulder straps.

When they reached eleven thousand feet, a green light above the door lit up. "Ready?" Liam shouted, and Lydia gave a barely perceptible nod. A man they hadn't met opened the door of the plane. A whoosh of air whipped through the cabin. The man grasped a bar outside the door and stood half in and half out of the plane. Liam and Lydia scooted up the bench to the door of the plane, and the man with the job Blake didn't envy helped them to a standing position. Lydia held the straps at her chest while Liam held the bar above the door. Blake and Buster moved up behind them.

"Just hold onto the straps and keep your head back," Buster yelled. "We'll be going right after them."

Blake nodded and watched Lydia. The wind pulled strands of her strawberry blonde hair loose, and they danced around her face. She turned to Blake and smiled, though it looked more like a grimace. "It was great meeting you," she yelled.

Blake grinned. "I hope we meet again," he yelled back.

Lydia leaned her head back into Liam's shoulder, and they were gone. Almost as soon as they'd jumped, the man standing on the precipice grasped Blake's hand, sports-team style and helped them up. The ground was more than two miles below. A few wispy clouds floated below them. Blake thought he might throw up, but the thought of losing his breakfast into the wind that was pelting his face made him steel his stomach. A second later, the light turned green, and Buster stepped out of the plane, Blake in front of him.

For a moment, Blake's body reacted with terror, sure he was hurtling to his death. The wind roared in his ears and cut off his air. His arms flailed for a moment, reaching for something stable. It was difficult to get a breath. Buster held his arms out above him, which reminded Blake to put out his arms and legs. Below him was a red speck. They fell faster than the speck and soon the speck became Lydia and Liam. Buster and Liam maneuvered through the air until they were about twenty feet apart. It looked like Lydia was yelling something, but Blake couldn't hear it above the roar of the air. She gave him a thumbs up, and Blake gave her one in return. Buster made an adjustment and they began a slow spin that took them farther away from Lydia. The ground below him was moving in circles as they fell fast.

Buster seemed to be in no hurry to pull the chute cord, and Blake started to wonder if he'd forgotten that little detail. "Don't forget to open the parachute," he yelled, but his words were probably lost in the screaming air.

Buster finally pulled the cord and the parachute opened above them. The sudden change in speed made Blake feel like a marionette whose puppeteer had experienced a sudden muscle spasm. Now they were falling feet first. The rumbling air quieted to a gentle whisper, and even though they were still falling much too quickly, the contrast was dramatic. It felt smooth and peaceful. Everything was intense and beautiful. From this vantage point he could see the city turn into suburbs, the suburbs into a patchwork of fields, and in the distance the fields gave way to the mountains. A few moments ago, the wind had robbed him of his breath. Now it was the beauty that stole it.

In the distance, Lydia waved as she swayed gently through the air. The earth seemed to move toward them faster the closer they got. "Hold your legs up," Buster said and Blake obeyed. Buster's feet hit the ground running and Blake remembered their safety briefing and kept his legs up and out of Buster's way.

When they were stopped and his feet were on the ground, his legs began to quiver as they adjusted to the earth's surface. Blake looked around for Lydia. She was landing about half a football field away. "Go find your girl," Buster said, when he'd unstrapped the parachute pack. "We'll get the rest of this off you inside."

Blake started toward Lydia on shaky legs. "That was the coolest thing I've ever done in my life," she yelled before he'd reached her. Liam was still unhooking her straps. "Did you like it?"

"Once the parachute came out. I could've done without the freefall."

When Lydia was free of the straps, she threw her arms around Blake's neck. "I loved it all," she said. Blake hugged her back, wishing they weren't wearing noisy nylon suits. "Thank you for making me do this." He put her down and she squealed again. "I can't believe we just did that."

The smile stayed on her face long after they were back in the car and driving toward Hickory. Blake felt a sense of pride that he'd helped put that smile there, and he kept glancing over at it. Something about her smile tugged at something inside him.

Five

She'd almost kissed him. Lydia couldn't believe she'd almost kissed him.

The crazy thing was, she'd just jumped out of an airplane, had watched the ground rise up to meet her, and all she could think about was that she'd nearly kissed Blake. It was probably because of the excitement of her first real adventure or the relief of having her feet solidly on the ground again. Or maybe it was her gratitude that Blake had arranged this whole wonderful, exhilarating experience. A doctor might have explained it away saying the fault belonged to the adrenaline coursing through her veins.

Whatever the cause, Lydia had hugged Blake and almost kissed him.

She blushed at the thought of it. It was so unlike her to be forward like that. Who was this girl who'd impulsively stayed in Charlotte and had just jumped out of an airplane? Lydia felt like she was in a stranger's skin.

"Hickory is the next exit. You'll turn right at the light." Blake had been pretty quiet since they'd gotten in the car.

She'd caught him glancing at her a couple of times, but he hadn't said much. "Are you glad you did it?" she asked him.

"I'm glad *we* did it," he said.

"Thank you. For doing that with me. I don't think I could have done it without you."

"That makes two of us."

"Turn left on 8th Street. It'll be on the left."

Blake pulled the car into the Shady Days Manor parking lot. The name was perfect. Large trees lined a wide sidewalk that led to the front doors of the gray stone building. The information desk looked like it belonged in the lobby of a fancy hotel. They stepped up to the counter and spoke to Candace, a girl with a sweet voice and heavy eyeliner.

"We're looking for a resident that lives here," Blake said. "Gladys Baker."

A sad expression came over the girl's face. "I'm so sorry. Gladys passed away last spring. I think it was in April." Blake took a slight step back, disappointment evident.

Lydia stepped closer to the counter. "Maybe you can help us." Lydia explained their situation to Candace. "Could you put us in touch with any family that might have taken her things? Could you possibly give us a phone number?"

"I don't think we can give that out. You'd need to talk to my supervisor, Janet. Maybe she can help you."

Janet was at lunch so they made an appointment to visit with her an hour later.

"They might not help us." Blake said as they ate tacos at a little restaurant a couple of blocks from Shady Days.

"Then we'll have to break into their offices after hours and find it ourselves."

"Wow. Get the unadventurous girl to jump out of an airplane, and she's suddenly ready to commit felonies. Criminals do lead adventurous lives, I suppose."

"Just show her that little dimple, and she'll probably give you whatever you want," Lydia said. Blake raised his eyebrows. Lydia couldn't believe she'd just said that out loud.

"I mean, just smile and be really nice to her and she'll probably cooperate. You know, be charming?" She wanted to crawl under the table. She really should have talked to more people the last three months. Maybe if she had, she wouldn't sound like a social buffoon.

"I'll do my best," Blake said, "but I'm afraid my charm has its limits."

Lydia wasn't sure about that.

Janet's stark office looked more like the showroom at an office furniture store. The only things on her desk were a computer screen and a telephone. A row of filing cabinets lined one wall, and a clock was mounted on the wall opposite the desk. There was nothing personal—no diplomas, no pictures, not even a nameplate.

"Please, come in." She motioned for them to take a seat and sat down opposite them. "Candace tells me you were asking about Gladys Baker."

Blake smiled a smile that would make an orthodontist proud, and Lydia bit the side of her mouth. "Yes, we've come from Denver. Gladys and my grandfather were friends. She had a box of belongings I was supposed to come get."

"But you're not actually related to her."

"No, but—"

"I'm terribly sorry, but our policy is that we don't give out any personal information. I'm sure you understand." She scooted away from the desk, ready to dismiss them.

"I understand, but Mrs. Baker told my grandfather to have me come."

"But Mrs. Baker is no longer here. Perhaps your grandfather knows Gladys's family and can arrange it for you."

"My grandfather died last spring. He can't arrange anything else."

"I'm so sorry. But I can't go against policy." Janet stood. "I wish I could help you."

"Ma'am, would it be possible for you to contact Gladys's family and see if they'd be willing to talk to us?" Lydia asked. Janet sat back down, a thoughtful look on her face.

"I could—"

The phone on Janet's desk buzzed, and a voice came over the intercom. "Janet, Grace Whittaker in Room 219 has fallen. Chet needs you up there right away."

"Of course," Janet said to the voice. "I'll be right there." She stood and ushered Blake and Lydia into the hall and closed the door behind her. "If you'd like to send me a letter, I'd be happy to forward it to Gladys's family. Now if you'll excuse me," she said and hurried down the hall.

"Great," Blake said as they started for the exit. "Now what would Nancy Drew do?"

Lydia watched Janet turn the corner and disappear. She stepped back and tried the door. It was unlocked. "She'd find a name," Lydia said. "Watch the door." Before Lydia could talk herself out of it, she was back in Janet's office.

"Lydia, I'm not sure this is a good idea," Blake said, but his words were lost as the door closed behind her.

"Baker. Baker." Lydia whispered as she opened the first file cabinet. It was hard to tell what these files were. Invoices? Payment records? Whatever they were, they were mostly numbers. Lydia closed the drawer and moved to the next cabinet. The top drawer started with the last name Andreason and then jumped right to Calloway. No Baker here.

And then the phone buzzed. Lydia froze. "Janet? Janet, could you please pick up? I have a delivery here for you. Janet?" a voice said through the speaker.

Lydia thought she might hyperventilate. She should leave. What if someone caught her in here? But she didn't want Blake's trip to be wasted, so she moved quickly to the third file cabinet. It was locked. It was probably Janet's purse or her private stash of chocolate.

She heard voices in the hall, but couldn't make out the words. Shadows moved in front of the frosted window in the door, and the voices continued. She was trapped here anyway. She might as well check the last file cabinet.

It was unlocked. The voices in the hall stopped as she quickly leafed through the files. Acord. Ashby. Atwood. Ball.

Baker, Gladys.

Lydia pulled out the file and looked over the first page. She flipped through the remaining pages, looking for the name of any next of kin. Nothing. Surely there was a name of some relative in here. She went back to the first page and examined it more slowly. There it was. Emergency contact: Francie Davis, Boone, North Carolina. Relationship: granddaughter. With shaking fingers, Lydia took a picture with her phone. She straightened the papers and carefully put the file back in the drawer.

"Let's go," she said to Blake who was waiting just outside the door. She quietly closed the door behind her.

Blake didn't speak. They walked into the lobby, careful not to rush. Lydia's legs felt weak and liquid. "Thanks for your help," Blake said to Candace.

"No problem. Y'all have a nice day."

The warm, outside air felt good. It meant that with every step, they were further from criminal charges. Blake unlocked her door for her. Lydia collapsed into her seat. Blake slid in behind the wheel and drove the car out of the parking lot.

"What did you just do?" Blake's voice was a tense whisper, and Lydia thought he might be angry.

"I just got her granddaughter's name and phone number."

"Lydia." His voice fell off, and she couldn't tell if he was annoyed or relieved. "I was joking about becoming a criminal."

"I know you were."

"Will she be able to tell you went through her things?"

Lydia took a ragged breath. "No. I was very careful. Who was in the hall?"

"A guy had a printing order. I talked to him for a minute and told him Janet was out of the office but I'd be sure she got it. It's on the floor just outside the door."

Blake pulled into the parking lot of a department store and put the car in park but left it running.

"Are you okay?" The concern in his voice made tears sting Lydia's eyes.

"Look at me. I can't stop shaking." She held her trembling hands up in front of her, and a tear slipped down her cheek.

"You're crazy," Blake said and pulled her into his arms. He rubbed her back, slowly replacing her frayed nerves with a wonderful tingling feeling.

"I've never done anything like that before," she said, her laughter accompanied by tears. Blake held her close as she calmed down. He smelled so good—citrusy and laundry soapy and manly.

"This won't be fun if I have to bail you out of jail. No more Nancy Drew stuff, okay?"

"Okay," she said into his shirt. When she finally pulled away, she dried her eyes. One of Blake's hands stayed on her back, like it was reluctant to leave. "I don't remember Nancy Drew ever saying how scary it was to be a detective."

Blake laughed and smoothed her hair, his hand barely touching her cheek.

"Tell me where we're going."

It was difficult to think of something other than the feel of his hand, but after a moment, she answered. "Boone."

Six

"Where is Boone?" Blake asked.

"I have no idea." Lydia's voice still had a little tremor in it, and Blake wished he was still holding her in his arms.

What had she been thinking? Sure, he was glad they had a name and phone number, but he'd stood out in that hall for several minutes imagining her going to jail. For him. He hadn't known what to do. Had he done the right thing by waiting and watching outside the door? What if Lydia had been caught? Should he have gone in after her and dragged her out?

What had happened to the bookworm he'd met at the airport yesterday?

"I'll get gas up here on the corner and you can figure out where Boone is."

"Sounds good." Lydia started digging through her purse. "Would you get me a bottle of water?"

"Of course. Put your purse away. I'll get it."

"You paid for the skydiving and my tacos. I don't want you paying for everything."

"A water is a lot cheaper than paying your bail. I've got this. You just figure out where we need to go."

"Boone is an hour north of here," she said when Blake came back to the car.

"It's already three. Maybe I should try calling her before we drive up there."

"Good idea. See if she can see us today, or if we should drive up first thing in the morning. Her name is Francie Davis."

Blake admired Lydia's positive attitude, but he wasn't sure if Francie would want to see them at all. He dialed the number Lydia gave him and the phone started to ring. He felt Lydia watching him as he waited for an answer. After five rings, it went to voicemail.

"My name is Blake Knowles. I'm trying to reach Francie Davis. My grandfather knew your grandmother. I'm in North Carolina and wondered if I could speak with you. Would you give me a call at your earliest convenience?" Blake left his phone number and hung up. Almost immediately his phone beeped with a text.

I can't talk. I'll call you back in about five minutes.

"I guess we wait," he said and drank most of his water. His fingers tapped on the steering wheel, releasing a little of his nervous energy. Lydia was leaning back on the headrest, her eyes closed. She looked drained.

Eight minutes later, Blake's phone rang. "Hello," he said on the first ring.

"Hi. This is Francie Davis. I just got your message."

"Thank you for calling me back. I came to Hickory to see your grandmother, but . . . I'm sorry for your loss."

"Thank you," Francie said. "What did you say your name was?"

"My name is Blake Knowles. Your grandmother and my grandfather were friends."

"Ah, yes."

"I guess my grandfather spoke to her about a year ago about a box. I don't know what's in the box, but he wanted me to have it, and Gladys, I mean your grandmother, said she had it and that I should come to North Carolina and get it." Suddenly Blake felt sick inside. What if Francie didn't have the box? And if she did have it, maybe she wouldn't want to give it to him. Would she question why it had taken him so long to come? How would he answer that? Sure, he'd been busy with his job, but that sounded like a hollow excuse now that Grandpa was gone.

It was quiet at the other end of the phone, and Blake wasn't sure if they were still connected. "Francie?"

"Yes, I'm still here."

"Is there any chance you might know something about the box? My grandfather's name was Elliott Knowles."

"Yes. I have it."

Francie didn't offer to let him come retrieve the box, and he felt uncomfortable asking for it. Then Blake thought of Lydia taking a risk to get him Francie's name. He thought of his grandfather in the hospital, hoping he'd made plans to go to North Carolina to get it, and he knew he couldn't fail. He took a deep breath and plowed on. "Would it be possible for me to come get it?"

He waited. It was probably only a few seconds, but the silence seemed to stretch on for minutes. He knew she was thinking, and something kept him from interrupting her thoughts. Finally, she spoke. "If your grandfather wanted you to have it, I won't keep it from you."

Blake slowly let out the breath he'd been holding. "Thank you. Like I said, we're in Hickory. We can be there in about an hour if that works for you." He looked at Lydia to see if he'd given the right length of time, and she nodded.

"I'm headed home right now. You can meet me there. Do you need the address?"

Blake repeated the address and Lydia entered it into her phone.

"Thank you, Francie. We'll see you soon."

Lydia put the address in her phone. "We need to get back out on the highway heading north."

Blake followed her directions, thinking about the phone call with Francie. They drove more than ten miles in silence before either of them spoke. "It didn't even occur to me until that phone call that I might be taking something important away from someone," Blake said. "She said she's willing to let me take it, but she sounded sad. I mean, think about it. This box and everything in it was her grandmother's for many years, and here's a stranger, out of the blue, asking for it."

"You don't have any idea what it is?" Lydia asked.

"No. I just know what Grandpa told me."

"What exactly did he say?"

The air started cooling as they drove into the mountains, and Blake turned the air conditioner down a notch. "I'd missed my mom's birthday dinner because of work. She said it was fine. She understood how busy I was, but I could tell she was disappointed. I stopped by their house the next Sunday to give her a birthday present, and Grandpa was there. He asked if we could go for a little walk. He said he was worried about me and asked me if I was busy with permanent things or temporary things. I told him my career felt like a pretty permanent thing." Blake looked at Lydia. She'd turned in the seat and was watching him as he spoke. He found her attention comforting.

"Grandpa said sometimes it's hard to tell what's permanent and what's temporary. He said because of his actions, something that should have been permanent became temporary. I asked him what he was talking about, and he said he had something he wanted me to have. Something he hoped would help me figure out the difference. And then he told me about Gladys and the box she was keeping for me.

"Almost every time I saw him, which wasn't often enough, he asked if I'd made plans to go get the box, and every time I told him, soon. I'll go soon. After he died, my dad gave me a folder from Grandpa. It has three letters from this Gladys woman that I'm supposed to read when I get the box and a letter from him to read after I've gone through everything in it. I've got the folder in my briefcase." Blake sighed and shook his head. "It still took me another four months to get out here and try to get it. He's probably so disappointed in me."

"He might have been, but I'll bet he's not now. Look at you. You'll have it in a little while, and you'll be able to see why it was so important to him."

"And I'm taking it from a woman who probably deserves it more than I do."

They were quiet for a moment. "Tell me about your grandpa," Lydia said.

"He was a very successful man. His family was poor, but he worked hard and put himself through college. He went to medical school in Boston then moved to Denver and took a position. He ended up staying there and eventually became the chief of staff at the biggest hospital in Denver."

"I guess success runs in the family. How did he meet your grandma?"

"Grandpa was much older than she was. He was pretty much a confirmed bachelor. Most people who knew him thought he'd never get married, but when he was almost forty, he met Grandma at a hospital Christmas party. She'd come as another doctor's date, but Grandpa couldn't take his eyes off her. When he found out the other doctor wasn't serious about her, Grandpa said he'd like to take her out. She was sixteen years younger than him, but they fell in love and got married the next summer. She died when my dad was nine. Grandpa never remarried."

"How sad for him."

"I know. As successful as Grandpa was, he always seemed a little sad. They were only married thirteen years."

"He must have really missed your grandma."

Blake felt tormented. His eyes were trained on the road, but his thoughts were a jumble. He thought of his grandfather in the hospital. He'd barely made it to see him before he died because Blake had been in a meeting that included two of the partners. Blake thought of Gladys, a woman who somehow fit into his grandfather's life, even though his father had never heard of her. Blake thought of the Challis-Austin merger and how Pryce Van Wagoner had probably reacted to his extended absence. He thought of this unusual girl who was afraid to face her friend and tell her she was unadventurous, but who had raided Janet's office to help him.

His cell phone interrupted the chaos of his thoughts.

"Hello."

"Blake," Brynn said. "Have you looked at your email?"

"I haven't had a chance."

"If you're going to skip out for two extra days, the least you could do is check your email."

"Sorry. What is it?" Blake's mind was now completely on work.

"Mary Challis is threatening to back out if we don't put her stock percentage back to 35 percent."

"That's only two percent more. Is she really willing to lose this whole deal for two percent?"

"If you were here, you could ask her that in one of her every-fifteen-minutes phone calls." Brynn was angry.

Blake sighed. "I thought we had these numbers squared away."

"Well clearly we don't. You need to call her. I hate to rain on your little treasure hunt parade, but if this falls through, you can pretty much kiss partnership goodbye. I called her and tried to calm her down, but she's upset. She said if she doesn't get the attention she deserves, she'll call another firm. This is big, Blake."

"I know it is."

"I forwarded Mary Challis's email to you. Two hours ago. If you're smart, you'll get on the phone and talk some sense into her. Sooner rather than later."

"Thanks, Brynn."

"Don't thank me. I'm just here at the office doing my job."

"I'll call her right now."

He hung up the phone. No matter what he did, he was letting someone down. By not going, he'd disappointed his grandfather. Now he'd left his firm in a bind. A headache was starting behind his eyes. "I've got to pull over at the next exit and make a phone call."

"Problems?"

Blake glanced over at Lydia's concerned face. He gave her a wry smile. "Yeah. Sixteen million of them."

Seven

lake took the next freeway exit, pulled off to the side of the road, and scrolled through his emails. Lydia watched his face change from concerned to panic-stricken in about two minutes. She wished she could offer some sort of support, but she didn't know how he'd react to her intruding on his thoughts, so she stayed quiet.

"Mary," he said after he dialed her number. "It sounds like we need to talk." He paused. "I can understand that. I thought you were happy with the numbers we'd worked out." Pause. "No, I didn't decide to take my vacation in the middle of your deal." Blake sighed. Back and forth they went for another ten minutes. Lydia could tell from Blake's side of the conversation that she was finally calming down. "All right, Mary. I'll see you at 8:30 on Wednesday. Don't worry about it between now and then. Everything's going to work out fine."

Blake hung up then called Brynn to give her the details of the phone call. A few minutes later, they pulled back onto the freeway.

"Sorry about that," he said.

"Sounds very stressful," Lydia said.

Blake rubbed the bridge of his nose, a move Lydia had seen every time he'd dealt with work. "Money can make people irrational."

"Then we'd better hope this box isn't filled with money," Lydia said.

Blake laughed. "Maybe I should have become a school teacher." He looked sheepish. "That was pretty thoughtless. I'm sure teaching a bunch of fifth graders is plenty stressful."

"It has its moments, but I think I'd rather deal with 28 fifth graders than be responsible for multimillion dollar deals. Most of the time, you can get a fifth grader to behave by promising them a brownie or an extra recess."

"Maybe I should take Mary a box of brownies Wednesday. Do you think that would help her see things clearly?"

"It depends on how much she likes brownies," Lydia said. "It would certainly help me see things more clearly. Oh, you need to get off the next exit."

Boone was a picturesque town in the Blue Ridge Mountains. The streets were blacktop stripes on a canvas that included every color of green from the darker shades of the trees and bushes to the lawns so saturated and bright they almost hurt your eyes.

"She lives a little outside of town," Lydia said. They passed a statue of Daniel Boone and three steepled churches before they turned east. The downtown district was charming and vibrant. Somehow it had avoided the forsaken, dilapidated condition of many older small towns. The brick and clapboard storefronts gave way to tidy old homes with neat yards. At the edge of town, occasional houses appeared tucked behind thick foliage. "I think it's that house right there," Lydia said.

At the top of a small knoll was a white, two-story farmhouse, complete with a covered, wraparound porch. "Nice place," Blake said.

"I love it. It looks like it belongs on a postcard."

They took the steps to the front door. The house was worn and in need of a fresh coat of paint, but that didn't rob it of its appeal. Blake knocked on the door.

A trim, dark-haired woman answered the door. Her high cheekbones and large eyes took her from unremarkable to interesting. "Come in," she said and held the door open. "I'm Francie."

"I'm Blake, and this is Lydia."

They followed Francie through an archway to what had probably once been called the parlor. Wood trim and walls gave it a rich feeling in spite of the dull paint and worn rugs. The furniture was old but clean. A cold, dark fireplace flanked with built-in wood bookshelves anchored one end of the small room. Books filled the shelves and several more were stacked on the coffee table.

"Please, sit down."

Blake and Lydia took two overstuffed chairs that faced the window. Francie sat in the corner of the couch and pulled her feet up underneath her. Late afternoon sunshine slanted through the room from behind her, making her expression impossible to read.

"Francie." A man's voice called from another room. "Francie, who is it?" His voice sounded urgent and irritated. Something fell and made a crashing sound.

"I'm sorry. My husband's in a wheelchair. I'd better make sure he's okay." Francie left the room, and they heard hushed voices for a minute before she returned.

"My grandmother never mentioned that someone would be coming to take her box of letters," Francie said as she walked back into the room. "Forgive my curiosity, but could you tell me again why I'm supposed to give them to you?"

Blake shifted in his chair uncomfortably and explained what his grandfather had told him. "I didn't know it was a box of letters. I just know my grandfather thought I needed what was in the box."

"There's more than just letters. There are other mementos in there, too. Including an engagement ring."

"I didn't know."

"I've read the letters and looked through the box. I'm not sure why your grandfather thought you should have it, but I suppose he had his reasons. Of course, I'm sad to part with them, but I don't want to go against their wishes."

"Thank you," Blake said. "I'm sorry to take—"

Francie held up her hand to stop him. "Please. All I ask is that, if you decide you don't want or need them anymore, I'd like them to come back to me."

"Of course," Blake said.

"I read in a book once that letters are a priceless part of someone's history. Too many people discard them without realizing what a treasure they are. I don't want them to be lost."

"I understand."

Francie left the room again. When she returned, she held an old shoe box with the words Enna Jettick on both ends. The cardboard corners were velvety with wear. "I'm guessing this is the box he meant. The letters are from Elliott to my grandmother." It was strange to hear this stranger call his grandfather by his first name.

"Thank you, Francie. I know it must be difficult turning these over to a stranger, but I promise you, I'll take good care of them."

Francie swallowed hard and gave a short nod. She didn't sit back down, so Lydia and Blake stood. Francie handed the box to Blake then moved to the front door.

"It was nice to meet you," Lydia said as she left. Blake shook Francie's hand, and they walked quietly to the car. Francie closed the door behind them.

Blake handed Lydia the box when they were in the car.

Neither of them spoke until they'd turned the corner off Francie's street.

"That was so sad," Lydia finally said, her hand over her heart.

"I felt terrible. I wouldn't have taken them if it hadn't been so important to Grandpa. It's like I was ripping her heart out. I hope this isn't all she has from her grandma."

"I'm sure it's not," Lydia said, trying to reassure him. "But I think these were special. She'd read them all."

"Thank you for coming with me, Lydia. It helped having you there."

Lydia ran her hand over the old shoe box on her lap. She resisted the urge to open it and look inside. It wasn't hers to look through.

Blake swung the car in a wide turn and headed back the direction they'd come. "I don't know if I can wait 'til we get back to the hotel. Let's get a piece of the world's best apple pie a la mode and take a look. He pulled the car into the side parking lot of a diner. The sign on the front actually said they served the world's best apple pie a la mode.

"That's a pretty bold claim," Lydia said.

"I'm not sure they can prove that, but it probably helps them sell pie," Blake said.

The diner was brightly lit, and the scent of apples and cinnamon gave credibility to the billboard. It smelled delicious. They requested a booth in the back and ordered two ice waters and two pieces of apple pie with vanilla ice cream.

"Let's wait and open it after we eat," Blake said. "I don't want to spill on anything." He put the box by the salt and pepper and sugar packets then pulled out his phone. "Sorry. I'd better be sure there hasn't been another crisis." He scrolled through his emails. The waitress brought them their pie and ice water. Blake ignored the pie while he typed into his phone.

Lydia took a bite and moaned. "I think the sign is accurate," she said.

"That good, huh?"

"Try it."

Blake finished his email and tucked his phone back in his pocket before he pulled his plate closer and took a bite.

"Wow," he said over the pie in his mouth. When he swallowed, he continued. "Definitely the best I've ever had."

"This is heavenly," Lydia said. "It's a good thing there's not one of these in Bridger. I'd be in trouble." She looked at Blake to see if he was enjoying the pie as much as she was. He was watching her, a small smile turning up the corner of his mouth. "What?" she said, wiping her mouth with a napkin.

"Nothing."

"Do I have food on my face?" she asked.

"Huh uh," Blake said, shaking his head.

"What then? Why are you looking at me like that?"

"Cause you're nice to look at." Lydia felt the color rise in her cheeks, and Blake's smile widened.

"Knock it off," she said. "Eat your pie."

"I am," he said, taking another bite. "I wasn't trying to embarrass you. Just calling it like I see it."

Lydia rolled her eyes. "Says the man who looks like a movie star." Blake shook his head. "Just calling it like I see it," Lydia said.

When the pie was gone, Blake stacked the plates and put them at the end of the booth. "Let's see what we've got here." He held the shoe box on the table in front of him. "I'm almost afraid to open it. Do you mind if I come sit by you, so we can look together?"

Was he kidding? "Of course I don't mind." Lydia scooted closer to the wall. Blake slid in beside her. Their legs were touching and his arm brushed hers as he moved, making it hard to think about the box or its contents. She could barely remember her name.

Blake slid the box so it was centered between them and

gently removed the lid. About twenty letters were bound together with a pale blue ribbon. The front envelope was postmarked Denver, 1947. The letter was addressed in a long, elegant cursive to Gladys Renari. Blake took the bundle out and placed it beside the box. Lydia pulled out a program from an orchestra concert at Boston University. The paper was yellowed and brittle. Blake leaned closer to look at it. "That must be from when he was in medical school," he said. Lydia put it beside the letters on the table.

The waitress brought a pitcher of water to refill their glasses. "No thanks," Blake said as he held up his hand to stop her. Blake moved the glasses to the edge of the table so she could take them. Next, he pulled out two tickets. "Look at this. Boston Celtics tickets from 1946. Grandpa said he was there for their first season. He never would cheer for the Nuggets. Always cheered for the Celtics." He handed the tickets to Lydia.

There was a small lavender and white striped box that said, "Griffin Shoe Wax." Blake opened the lid and tipped its contents into his hand. It was a dried rose. It had probably been red at one time, but now it was a deep russet color. He put the rose back in the box and handed it to Lydia.

Next, he brought out two black and white photographs. "Is that your grandpa?" Lydia asked, leaning in a little closer.

"Yes." Blake turned the first picture over.

"Elliott Knowles and Gladys Renari. 1946," Lydia read. They were standing, arms around each other, smiling in front of a sleek, two-door Studebaker. The second picture showed Blake's grandpa in a graduation cap and gown, Gladys standing proudly beside him.

"They look really happy," Lydia said.

The last thing Blake pulled out was a small fabric bag. Inside was a gold filigree ring with a single, small diamond in the center. Blake sighed and slid down in his seat. "What did he want me to have all this for?" he said, more to himself than to Lydia.

"Maybe it's in the letters."

Blake leaned his head back against the seat and rubbed his temples. "I'm tired."

Lydia turned sideways in her seat to face him. "It's been a long day." Blake was sitting so close she could see the little lines around his eyes. His dark hair brushed the top of his ears. She was surprised how much she wanted to touch it.

"Hard to believe we jumped out of a plane this morning. It feels like that was a month ago," he said turning his head toward her.

"Plus your worries about work. And this." She gestured toward the mementos spread out on the table. "No wonder you're tired. Do you want me to drive?"

"Do you mind?" he asked.

"Not at all." Lydia carefully put everything back in the box. As she put on the lid, Blake dug in his pocket and put a few bills on the table. He put out his hand and helped her out of the booth, then picked up the box and followed her out. Lydia wished her hand was still in his.

Eight

"Look at that sky," Lydia said when they walked out of the diner. Pink and orange clouds made ribbons that slashed the darkening blue sky. "It's beautiful. Pink clouds at night, sailor's delight. My dad used to say that. Not sure what the rest of it is."

"I guess tomorrow's going to be a good day," Blake said. He handed Lydia the car keys.

"Can't be much better than today. With the exception of the problems at your job," she said.

"And hopefully tomorrow I won't have to worry about you committing a felony."

"I promise. I'll be good."

"You'd better. Aren't you supposed to set a good example for your students? Good citizenship, right?"

"Right. I'll tell them about skydiving, but I won't tell them about Janet's office."

The trees around them turned from green to black and stars appeared as they drove toward Charlotte. "Tell me about you," Blake said. Lydia giggled. "I'm serious."

"What do you want to know?"

He wanted to know everything, but saying that would probably scare her. "Whatever you want to tell me."

"Okay." Lydia looked self-conscious. "I've lived in Colorado all my life. I have an older brother, Jace. I graduated from Colorado State, and this is my second year of teaching school. I live with my Grandpa. And I like to read. But you already know that."

"What makes you happy?"

"That's a Barbara Walters question. What makes *you* happy?"

"You first."

"You just want me to sound corny."

"I'm sure I'll sound corny, too," Blake said.

"Hmm. What makes me happy? A good book. Yellow flowers, especially tulips. Good music. I really like the old-fashioned stuff like Frank Sinatra and Johnny Mathis. Don't laugh," she said, laughing.

"I'm not the one laughing."

"But I know you want to."

"No, I don't. Keep going," he said.

"Cute notes from my students. And waterfalls. I have a thing for waterfalls. I love the way they sound and the mist on my face. Oh, and skydiving. That made me happy. Your turn. What makes you happy?"

Blake thought for a moment. "Sundays. I like Sundays because it's the one day I probably don't have to work."

"Probably? You actually have to work some Sundays?"

"When you're trying to make partner, you work whenever there's something that needs done. Most weeks I put in over eighty hours."

"Blake, that's not even good for you," Lydia said and he could tell she said it out of concern and not judgment. "No wonder you like Sundays. So what else? Makes you happy, I mean."

"My nephew, David. He's two. He calls me Bake. And my mom's pineapple upside down cake."

"Mmm. That sounds good."

"It is. I like golf. I used to play a lot with my dad. I don't really have time now, but someday I'll play again. I even like watching it. And skydiving doesn't really make me happy."

"Really?"

"Watching you skydive made me happy, but I don't think I'd ever do it again. I prefer to be inside the plane or on the ground."

"So I guess you're probably not interested in bungee jumping with me?"

Blake laughed. "Probably not. I'll watch you though, if you want to jump."

"I'm just kidding. I'd be afraid my cord would snap."

"But you weren't afraid the parachute wouldn't open?"

"Of course I was. I know. It's ridiculous. I guess it was less scary because if the bungee cord broke, I'd have no time to figure out how to survive. It'd just be, splat, you're dead. But jumping out of a plane, if the parachute didn't open, there'd be more time to figure out how to try to live through it."

"Yeah. Ridiculous. You'd just have more time to think about dying."

Lydia laughed. "Maybe it just sounds better because I'd have more time to confess all my sins before I died."

"You have sins?"

"Don't we all?"

"I'm sure we do, but I can't really picture you with any great vices."

"Maybe that's because you don't know me very well."

"Maybe." It was strange to think that he'd known her for such a short time. It felt like they'd been friends forever.

They talked all the way back to Charlotte.

"You want to share a pizza?" Blake asked in the elevator. "I need something besides apple pie for dinner, and I thought maybe we could read a few of these letters tonight."

"Sure."

Blake ordered a pizza while Lydia laid the letters out according to postmark. After he hung up the phone, he retrieved a folder from his briefcase. "Here are the three letters she sent to Grandpa," Blake said, taking them from the folder and handing them to Lydia. She checked the postmarks and placed them in order.

"Here's the first one. March 4, 1947. Do you want to read it?"

"You go ahead," Blake said.

Lydia sat cross-legged on the bed. Blake sat back against the headboard, his hands behind his head.

> *My dearest Gladys,*
>
> *I arrived on Friday night. The trip was uneventful except for a flat tire and a heavy snowstorm. I was grateful the flat tire didn't happen during the storm. I made good time and the car proved to be reliable. The biggest problem I encountered on the trip wasn't the storm or the tire, however. It was my loneliness for you. I had too many hours to miss you and wish you were with me.*
>
> *I'm sharing an apartment with three other doctors. They're all fairly new. The old-timer of the bunch has only been here for fourteen months. They're pleasant fellows. Harvey is from Palo Alto, California. Silas is from Gilbert, Arizona and John is from Spokane, Washington. I'm the only one from east of the Mississippi. I thought we might share meals, but they said we're rarely here at the same time, so we each cook for ourselves. I hope I don't starve.*
>
> *Denver is larger than I thought it would be. I thought it was in the mountains, but the mountains are actually off in the distance. I drove to them today. It took me more than half an hour.*

I start working tomorrow. I'm excited to be a real doctor. There were many times I wondered if this day would arrive. Knowing we'll be married within a year gives me the will to succeed. I want to buy you a beautiful house and take you out to fine restaurants.

Lydia looked up at Blake. "Blake, you don't have to share these with me. I'd totally understand if you want to just read them yourself."

"No. This is good. Keep going. We'll take turns reading them." Blake didn't want to do this alone. He wanted to share it with her. He was already learning more about his grandfather's life than he'd known before, and there was something reassuring about sharing it with someone else, sharing it with Lydia. She continued reading.

It's been less than a week and I miss you so much it hurts. It's a physical pain in my heart and the only antidote will be letters and occasional phone calls. I miss your brown eyes. I miss your smile. I miss your laughter. I miss you calling me Dr. Knowles. I could go on and on, but I'd rather not have my roommates walk in and catch me crying like a baby.
I love you.
Yours, Elliott.

The second letter was much like the first. They read several more letters. Each was full of love and excitement for the future. Most shared some of his experiences at the hospital. Some were funny stories, some sad, but all made Blake feel closer to his grandpa.

It was Blake's turn to read, so he picked up the next letter. He bent his legs and propped his forearms on his knees as he started to read.

"This one is postmarked August 28, 1947."

My Dearest Gladys,

It was with heavy heart that I read your last letter. I'd hoped we'd be getting married in December when I came home for Christmas. Hearing that you feel we should wait a little longer was a devastating disappointment. I don't understand why you want to put it off.

Let me reassure you of a few things. First, I hope you feel confident in my love for you. You're my world and I won't know true happiness until we're together. Second, I'm doing my best to become established so you'll feel confident in my position. I want my job to be secure and I want to buy you a beautiful home. I want to provide for you and our children. I don't ever want you to have to worry about money. I want you to be a doctor's wife who can go to lunch with friends and belong to the country club.

If you have doubts about marrying so soon, please consider moving to Denver so we can spend more time together. We could rent a room for you and we'd be close to each other. That would make courting much easier, don't you think? We could begin looking for a house to buy. In the spring, we could marry in Charlotte and return as husband and wife.

Please say you'll come.
Yours always,
Elliott

The pizza had arrived while Blake was reading so when he finished the letter, they took a break and ate. Then Lydia opened the next letter and began reading.

October 12, 1947
Dear, Dear Gladys,

I've been floating on air ever since I got your last letter. Even a little boy with a broken arm that wouldn't stop screaming couldn't dampen my spirits. He was crying and crying and it took two nurses and both his parents to hold him down so we could plaster it, but I just felt like whistling a tune. I had to work at making my face look solemn, and I'm afraid I wasn't entirely successful because at one point his father said, 'Why are you smiling? This is terrible for him.' Of course I wasn't smiling about his pain. I was smiling because you're coming.

You're coming. You're coming. We'll be together soon. John says I'm turning his stomach with my endless crowing. His girl is in Gilbert, and he wishes she could come.

It will be wonderful having you here. I looked in the paper and saw there was a job for a telephone operator for Mountain Bell and a file clerk at the Denver City Hall. I'm sure you'll be able to find a position.

I hope your parents are warming to the idea. I can certainly understand how they'll miss you. I've been living without you for seven months now, and I don't want it to go on a moment longer. Tell them I'm working hard so they'll see what a good provider I'll be for their daughter.

I stopped by Chandler's Boarding House on my last day off and spoke to a woman named Eloise. She said she'll have an opening in November. I gave her a $25 deposit and $45 for November's rent. I think you'll like it there. It's a lovely house, and it includes dinner. She said the décor in your room is pale green. I thought that was perfect for you.

My beautiful Gladys will be here in just weeks.

Soon I'll be holding you in my arms, and we'll be planning our wedding. I look forward to your arrival.

I love you with all my heart,
Elliott

Blake reached for the next letter.

December 6, 1947
Dear Gladys,
I still don't know what happened. I went by
Chandler's to see you Friday afternoon and
discovered you were gone. I called your house on
Saturday, but your mother said you hadn't arrived
home yet. I'm trying to be understanding, but I'm
hurt and angry.

"Oh no," Lydia said. "What happened?"
Blake continued to read.

I can't believe you left with no goodbye and no
explanation. I had to find out from Eloise Chandler.
I've read your note again and again. As hard as I'm
working for us, for you, I don't understand how you
could call me selfish. You say you'd rather have me
work at a factory than see so little of me. That's easy
to say now, but what about when you want a new
dress or a nicer car? What about the beautiful house
we've dreamed of and planned for? I've never wanted
to provide you with the lifestyle that would come
from common labor. That's why I took this job. I'm
working all these hours for us, and you call me selfish
and leave without a word.
I'm sorry you felt lonely. I never want you to feel
lonely, but please think of me. I've been here for nine
months and most of it has been spent lonely and
missing you. But I'd happily put up with all of it in
order to give us the best possible life. When I asked
your father for your hand, he told me he wanted the

best for his daughter. I want the best for his daughter, as well.

Please come back. None of this is worth it without you. Just be patient. It won't always be like this.

Love,
Elliott

"Poor Elliott," Lydia said. "He's so hurt and angry." Blake leaned back his head and closed his eyes. "It's after midnight, Blake. Do you want to finish these in the morning?"

"No," he said, his eyes still closed. "We're almost finished. Unless you're too tired, of course." A solemn mood had fallen over the room. Both of them knew sadness was imminent, and they spoke a little softer, a little more carefully. "Would you read them?" Blake asked. He ached for the loneliness his grandfather had felt, the loss he'd endured. Lydia's voice was soothing and the painful reproach he felt was coming would be easier to endure wrapped in her gentle delivery.

"Yes."

"Thank you."

Lydia opened the next letter. "This one is from December 26, 1947."

Darling Gladys,

Christmas just wasn't Christmas without you. I didn't know if I'd hear from you, so I was surprised and pleased when I received your gift. I hope this means we're not finished. I opened your present before I went to work at midnight Christmas Eve. Thank you for the lovely gifts. As you can see, I'm writing on the stationery you sent. The "Dr. Elliott Knowles" at the top of the page could only be improved if it said "Dr. and Mrs. Elliott Knowles." I wore the bowtie to work just to remind me of you.

This was the week I thought we'd be getting married. But instead, I'm here in Denver and you're back in Charlotte with your family. I miss the days when I was doing my residency and you were going to school. I never imagined that I'd look back on my residency and long for it again. I'm still hopeful that this will be my last Christmas alone, that we'll be together next year in our own home, with a tree we decorated together and our own snowy front yard, complete with a snowman like the one we built in Boston.

Yesterday was difficult in many ways. A family that was traveling to visit their grandmother for Christmas dinner ended up in the emergency room after a terrible car accident. The roads were icy and their car went off the road and turned over onto its roof. What a sad way to celebrate the holiday. Even sadder, their three-year-old daughter didn't survive. Christmas will forever be ruined for them. We tried our best to save her, but there was nothing we could do. I cried in front of Dr. Tate. He's an older doctor who's been here for nearly thirty years. I felt terrible and told him I was sorry for being so unprofessional, and he put his hand on my shoulder and said," The most unprofessional thing we can do is stop feeling joy and grief with our patients." It made me feel a little better.

I wish I could come home at night to you instead of to three men. Silas snores and John's feet smell so bad that sometimes I walk in the apartment and the stench nearly knocks me back out the door. It makes me miss the scent of your rose perfume.

I love you, Gladys, and hope we still have a

future together.
   All my love,
   Elliott

Blake was quiet when Lydia finished the letter. He felt strangely exposed. Lydia hadn't been there for all the missed family events. She hadn't been affected by the long work days that often stretched into night. These were things he'd rather she didn't see, especially in this context. Blake wanted to rationalize it away, just as his grandfather had tried to do in these letters. He wanted to defend himself from what felt like an accusation from beyond the grave. He didn't want Lydia to think less of him.

The thing that kept him quiet was the knowledge that his grandpa had loved him. He'd sent Blake to find this box because he had thought it would teach him something. He couldn't ignore it, even if it made him uncomfortable. What he'd do with it, he wasn't sure.

Blake looked at Lydia. She was leaning over the letters, carefully putting the ones they'd read back in the box. Her strawberry blond hair fell in front of her face, and she tucked it behind her ear. Blake resisted the urge to pull her close to him, to touch her face, to hold her hand. She probably wouldn't want him to. She was reading these letters and seeing what Elliott had done to his relationship. She knew Blake was like his grandfather, that he'd made the same mistakes as Elliott. He had put work before family. He'd let his job keep him from this message from his grandfather. Blake felt a strange sadness that this thing that had started with Lydia, whatever it was, was probably over before it had even begun.

Nine

Blake was visibly upset, and Lydia didn't know what to do about it. She couldn't gloss it over. These letters were a message from his grandfather, a lesson he'd felt was important enough to send Blake across the country. To tell him it was no big deal and everything was fine would be to undermine his grandfather, and she wouldn't do that.

"Do you want to read now or would you like me to keep going?" she asked quietly.

"Could you?" he asked.

"Yes. The next two are from Gladys's to Elliott. Do you want me to read them in order or just finish his?"

"Let's finish them all."

"Okay. Gladys wrote this to Elliott on January 22, 1948."

Dear Elliott,

I know how disappointed you are, and I hate being the cause, but I'm just so torn. I love you so much and can't picture my life with anyone but you, but I also can't picture my life living so far from my family and being married to someone who's never home.

I know it's hard for you to understand. You're a man, and you had no trouble picking up your life and moving to a faraway city, but you've got your job. You're at work every day doing important things like saving people's lives. The month I was there was the loneliest month of my life. I think I missed you even more while I was there than I had when I was here in Charlotte. At least when I was here, there was a reason to miss you. There, it felt like I should see you more than just a few scattered hours here and there.

Maybe I'm just immature and childish. Maybe you were right when you called me spoiled and selfish, but I can't help how I feel. I was terribly hurt when you'd take extra shifts when you could have been with me. Over and over, Eloise called me to the phone so you could tell me you wouldn't be coming by because you'd picked up another shift. I just kept thinking the people you were working for were going home and you weren't. It wasn't what I expected when I came to Denver, and I was miserable.

I love you, Elliott Knowles, and I know you love me. I just don't know if I want to live with the kind of love you want to give me. I don't know if I want to have children whose father is gone when they get up and doesn't come home until long after they're in bed. It hurts me to say these things to you. I'm sorry.

Gladys

Blake's face looked pained. Lydia wanted to be done with it, but she didn't want to leave him to finish alone, so she hurried to the next one. "This one is also from Gladys. She wrote it on April 24, 1948."

Dear Elliott,

I don't know how to tell you this without it breaking your heart, but I've met someone. It's still pretty new, and I don't know where it will lead, but I don't want to keep secrets from you. He's not as handsome as you, although he is pleasant enough, and he'll never be as successful as you will be. I know if I marry him, I'll be giving up many of the things you wanted to give me, but I think I'm fine with that. He works at an insurance company. It isn't fancy work, but he leaves it behind at the end of the day and is home every night before six. It's a stable job, and a family with him would be more like my family was, more like the family I've always wanted.

My heart breaks when I think of you. I don't know if I'll ever feel like I did when we were together. You'll probably say I'm settling for less than I should, and maybe I am, but I feel comfortable and peaceful, and I'm not lonely.

I do hope you're well. You're in my thoughts every day.

I'm sorry, Elliott.

Gladys.

"Just two left. This one is from Elliott. June 19, 1948."

Dear Gladys,

I haven't heard from you for a while, so I decided to give myself a birthday present and call you on June 17. Your mother said you were on your honeymoon.

I don't know what to say. I didn't know things had progressed to that point. I know it has been a long time since I've heard from you, but I still had hopes that eventually you'd come back to Denver. I still pictured a happily ever after for us, but I guess that's not to be.

I still don't understand why you didn't want what I had to offer, but I'll do my best to accept things as they are. I don't know if I'll ever love someone the way I love you. I fear I'll love you and miss you every day of my life.

Be happy and have a good life.
Elliott

"This is the last letter," Lydia said. "It's from Gladys. It's dated July 9, 1948."

Dear Elliott,

Mother didn't tell me you called on your birthday until after I received your last letter. I'm sorry you found out I was married that way. That was very unkind of me. I just didn't know how to tell you.

Elliott, please try to understand. I wanted to be someone's world, and I think your world is your hospital.

I hope you find someone wonderful and that you have a happy life. I pray you don't hate me.
Gladys

Lydia folded the letter and put it back in the envelope. Blake's eyes were closed, his head propped up on pillows against the headboard, and his fingers laced across his stomach. She'd thought he was attractive when she'd first met him at the airport, but tonight he looked even better. He still looked like a movie-star, but there was more to him now. His long legs stretched the length of the bed. If she reached out her hand, she could touch them. He had good hands, long and lean, but strong. They'd encouraged her on their skydive, they'd comforted her after they left Shady Days.

Right now there was no dimple. Worry lines etched his forehead. Lydia wished she could wipe them away. Tonight hadn't been easy for him. The message from his grandfather, a man he loved and admired, was pretty clear, and it cast a shadow over Blake and his entire life. That had to have been hard to hear. She wanted to offer him comfort but there wasn't much she could say. She could only hope these letters would help Blake avoid the heartbreak his grandfather had endured.

Lydia moved to the end of the bed, careful not to bounce the mattress. "I'm not asleep," Blake said, opening his eyes. "Just thinking."

Lydia looked at him, and his eyes held hers. An ache started deep inside her and wrapped itself around her heart. Maybe he felt it too, or maybe they were just too tired to drag their eyes somewhere else, but even though the look lasted longer than should have been comfortable, neither of them looked away.

"Are you okay?" Lydia whispered.

Blake gave a small nod. "Not a very happy ending."

"It's heartbreaking," she said. Blake's eyes moved to her lips. Only then did Lydia look down at her hands, color rising in her cheeks.

"Come on. I'll walk you to your room," Blake said.

Lydia struggled to keep her breathing steady as she followed Blake to the door. He grabbed his keycard and her purse off the dresser and held the door open above her head. She ducked under his arm, and the door swung shut behind them.

Lydia pulled her keycard out of her bag, but instead of unlocking the door, she turned to Blake. "Do you think he regretted not going after her?"

Blake shrugged and leaned a shoulder against the wall. "I don't know. Maybe it was too late to change her mind. Even if he'd been willing to change."

"Are you glad you found the box, or do you wish you hadn't?" She wanted him to feel okay about it. She'd suggested he stay. Maybe it would have been better if he'd boarded that plane and never found out about the doomed relationship between Elliott and Gladys. But that would have meant their time together wouldn't have happened, and Lydia almost couldn't bear that thought.

Blake smiled. He reached up and tucked a strand of hair behind her ear. His fingers brushed against her cheek, sending shivers down her back. Then his hand traveled slowly to her shoulder and down her arm until he took her hand and held it in his. "It was hard to read, but I feel closer to Grandpa, and I understand him better." His thumb moved over the back of her hand. She watched his face as he looked down at their hands. His strong jaw with a day's scruff and the small scar on his chin. She noticed a tiny freckle on the side of his nose.

And suddenly Lydia wanted more than to hold his hand. She wanted more time than tomorrow. She wished they could stay suspended here forever.

"I'm not sorry at all," Blake said, meeting her eyes. His gaze moved to her lips and Lydia thought he might kiss her, but then Blake squeezed her hand and let it go. He smiled back at her before they entered their separate rooms. "I'll see you in the morning, Lydia."

Ten

Blake brushed his teeth slowly. He wanted to think about Lydia. She was charming and sweet and bashful. He wanted to picture her cute nose, scrunching up when she laughed. He wanted to think about their day and imagine kissing her goodnight instead of lamely saying he'd see her in the morning.

The problem was that his mind kept getting trapped in his grandfather's tragedy. He couldn't stop thinking about the pain his grandfather had endured because of his relentless pursuit of his career. Even though part of him felt disloyal to the grandmother he'd never known, Blake couldn't help feeling sad for Elliott and Gladys and the loss of their dreams. Had his grandfather been wrong? Maybe, but Blake understood his motivation, his drive to be successful. He loved the feeling that came with success, the rush when he handled a case successfully. He wanted to be free of financial worries.

Blake opened his briefcase and took out the letter his grandfather had written to him. He probably should have read it with Lydia. She'd just lived through Elliott and

Gladys's entire doomed relationship, after all. But he worried the letter might hold too strong a reproach and he wasn't sure he wanted to be scolded in front of her. He turned on the lamp and got into bed.

The letter was three hand-written pages. After reading so many letters in his grandfather's youthful hand, it was surprising to see the shaky lines of an elderly man. The letterhead said "Dr. Elliott Knowles" at the top. It was identical to the letterhead he'd used after Christmas all those years ago.

> *Dear Blake,*
>
> *I hope since you're reading this, that you've met Gladys and read the letters I sent her. I thought hearing the words of my thirty-year-old self would have more impact than the words of an old man saying "slow down" or "you work too much."*
>
> *Before I go any further, it's important that I tell you that I loved your grandmother with all my heart. She saved me. I was a broken, lonely man and somehow your grandmother put me back together. She gave me your father and you and your brother. She brought me laughter and joy and love. She was my world.*
>
> *But Gladys was my first great love. I met her in the fall of 1945. I was a resident at Boston Medical Center, and Gladys came to the emergency room with her roommate. They were students at Boston College and her roommate (I don't remember her name) had cut her hand fixing dinner and needed stitches. I took care of her friend, but Gladys is the one that caught my eye.*
>
> *When I lost her, I thought I'd lost it all. For many years, I thought she'd destroyed me. It wasn't until I was almost forty years old that I realized I'd destroyed myself. I spent years telling myself I was*

noble and good because I was so devoted to my work. But I wasn't noble and good. I was selfish and arrogant. I told myself I wanted to be successful because of what it would let me do for those I loved, but when I looked at my heart, I knew I was doing it for me. Those I loved would have been perfectly happy even if I hadn't become the Chief of Staff. Gladys married an insurance salesman who made less than half what I did, and she went on to have a happy life.

Blake, your father wasn't like me. He's a successful man and a good provider, but he was never driven to work the way I was. Neither is Pete. They've both found balance in their lives. But you aren't like them, my dear grandson. Sadly, you're too much like me. I see you breaking your back, putting in ridiculous hours, missing important things, permanent things, all so you can be successful, so you can become a partner and make more money.

Please stop. Let this old man teach you a lesson while you're still young enough not to be ruined by the drive that almost ruined me. It doesn't matter if you're a partner. I know you think it does, but it doesn't. You're sacrificing permanent things—family, memories, peace—for temporary things—accolades, money, power. Those things don't make you happy, Blake, and when you're an old man, you'll realize how empty they are.

You're on a path that leads to disappointment, and you're running as fast as you can. If you keep going down that path, you'll surely reach it.

I hope when you meet Gladys, you'll recognize what I gave up. I hope when you read my letters, you'll see some of the pain I caused Gladys and myself. I was angry at her for a long time, but she did the right thing by leaving me. A good woman doesn't want or deserve what I was trying to give. A good woman just wants a good man and a happy family.

Be a good man, Blake. Find a good woman. Love her. Work to provide for your family, not for honors and accolades. The people telling you what you're worth at your office would gladly rob you of the joy of pushing your child on a swing. The clients you devote your life to won't make you soup when you're sick and go grocery shopping with you. They won't sleep beside you at night. Don't live your life for the wrong people.

And most of all, don't confuse the worth of a career with the worth of relationships. Your career will never deserve more of you than the people you love who love you back. Don't learn these lessons the hard way.

I love you, Blake. It's my family that made my life worth something.

Love,

Grandpa Knowles

The letter sounded just like Grandpa. The words pierced Blake in his heart. He wiped his eyes and put it away. Grandpa had said he and Blake were the most alike. It was true. Blake had always looked up to him, had channeled his drive as he went through school and started at the firm. But after reading the letters tonight, Blake felt both honored and scared. Grandpa had been a good man, but his wisdom had taken time and had cost him plenty of heartache. He'd wasted many years and hurt people, including himself, before the wisdom came.

Blake turned off the light, but he didn't fall asleep. He thought of Lydia who slept on the other side of the wall. He'd only known her for two days, but it felt like so much longer. It had been a long time since he'd allowed himself to be interested in a woman. He'd figured he'd do that after he made partner. But what if the right woman was here now?

Blake felt sick inside. Even though he might be interested in Lydia, why would she give him a second thought? She'd just spent the last few hours reading letters that let her know exactly why she should turn and run from Blake. Gladys had showed Lydia what it took to find happiness. It took leaving.

He wasn't sure how to do it, but Blake wanted to make his grandpa proud of him. He wanted balance and peace, but he wasn't sure how to create it. Tomorrow, he'd spend the day with Lydia, but what about Wednesday when Brynn and Mary Challis and David Austin and Pryce Van Wagoner and a dozen other people made their demands? Once he tore himself into chunks and gave everyone their piece, what would be left for anyone else? Probably nothing worth having.

He and Lydia had one more day. One more day for him to enjoy her smile and share a laugh. One more day for adventure. One more day before the real world charged in and took them hostage. Blake got up and opened his laptop. After a quick search, he wrote down an address and phone number. When he got back in bed, he was finally able to fall asleep.

Shortly after eight the next morning, Blake was packing up his toiletries when he heard a soft knock on the door. "Good morning," he said when he opened it to Lydia.

"Oh good. You're up. We got to bed so late, I didn't want to bother you if you were still sleeping," she said.

"Funny. I thought the same thing. If you weren't up, I was just going to bring you back a muffin and some juice."

"So you haven't gone down to breakfast yet?" she asked, looking at his bare feet.

"Not yet. Let me put on some shoes, and we can go down together."

Lydia stepped into his room and let the door close behind her, but didn't come any farther inside.

She looked beautiful today. Her hair hung in loose waves that grazed her collarbone, her green peasant dress fit perfectly. "Nice dress," he said, his voice teasing.

"So it's okay if I wear this today?" she asked.

"It's certainly okay with me. But do you think you could wear those close-toed shoes you wore yesterday?"

Lydia groaned. "Are you serious?"

Blake laughed. "Yep. The dress is great, but we can't wear sandals."

"What are we doing today?" Lydia looked suspicious, and Blake laughed.

"Don't worry. Nothing like jumping out of a plane."

"Is it a secret, or do I get to know the plan?"

"It's not a secret. I'll tell you while we're eating."

When they were sitting at a table in the breakfast room, waffles and fruit in front of them, Blake told her his plans. "I booked us a Segway Lunch tour. It sounds fun. It's a two hour tour around the city and it finishes up with stops at three restaurants—one for an appetizer, another for an entrée and dessert at the last one. Have you ever ridden a Segway before?"

"I ride one to school every day." Her face was serious.

Blake looked surprised. "Really?"

"No, I'm not serious and no, I've never ridden one before. Have you?"

"We went to Washington, D.C. after I graduated, and my family took a Segway tour around the monuments. It's fun. I think you'll like it."

"Are they hard to ride?"

"No. It takes a few minutes to get comfortable on them, but they're easy."

"Thanks, Blake. This sounds like the perfect way to finish out our last day," Lydia said.

"Our last day in Charlotte, anyway," Blake said. The color that rose in Lydia's cheeks and the little smile she tried to hide gave Blake a good feeling about the return to Denver.

After breakfast, Lydia changed shoes, and they checked out of the hotel.

Eleven

ydia couldn't believe this was the same Charlotte she'd lived in for the last three months. She'd seen so little of the city during her time here. "I feel like a prisoner who's finally been set free," she said to Blake. "Look at all these things I've missed out on."

"You're not missing out today," he said. "Keep track of what you really like. Maybe you'll come back here someday, and you'll have a head start."

Lydia smiled at his encouraging words, but she was even more upset with herself now. No wonder Cambri had loved it here. It was a beautiful city.

Jamal, their guide, led them down tree-lined streets, pointing out historic homes and buildings. They rode through Fourth Ward Park, past the Settler's Cemetery and through the business district.

The tour was made up of Blake and Lydia and a family of four from Memphis. The teenage children were precocious and had elaborate questions for the guide. Lydia wondered if they were really curious or if they just enjoyed trying to stump the guide and see their parents nod admiringly.

Blake and Lydia didn't mind the questions. Sometimes they pulled their Segways up close and listened to the conversations and sometimes they lagged back and had their own.

Lydia loved riding the Segway. When they'd arrived for the tour, their guide had given each of them a helmet and a quick rundown of how they worked. Then they'd followed him to a flat, grassy area where Lydia had practiced until she felt comfortable. The subtle body movements it took to move forward and maneuver the machine felt like something out of a science fiction movie. Lydia got the hang of it pretty quickly. Blake already knew what he was doing, so he'd stepped out of the practice area and returned calls to Brynn and Mary Challis. They hadn't been easy phone calls and it had taken the first half of the tour for the worry lines to leave his forehead.

"Now we're to the good part," Jamal said. "The food. This is Charlie's. He came to the United States twenty-four years ago from Hong Kong. When he got here, he worked at a clothing factory, and every day he'd bring a lunchbox of homemade potstickers. They musta smelled amazing 'cause his co-workers started paying him to bring them potstickers for their lunch. Before long, Charlie was bringing a giant kettle of potstickers and selling them for a dollar each. He was making more during lunch than he was the rest of the day working on the line. That's when his wife, who was helping him make potstickers every night, suggested they'd make more money if they opened a little restaurant. Charlie's makes a whole lot more than potstickers now, but they're still what he's most famous for. People come from all over North Carolina for his potstickers. So that's what we're having for our appetizer course—Charlie's potstickers."

They lined up the Segways outside of Charlie's and sat at a long table inside. Charlie came from the kitchen, bowing. His smile seemed larger than his face. "Welcome, welcome," he said, his hands clasped in front of him as he bowed. "So glad you come to Charlie's. Where you from?"

"Memphis," the father of the family said, waving his hand in a circle to distinguish the four of them.

"Veyee good, veyee good." Charlie turned to Blake and Lydia. "And you from?"

"We're from Denver," Blake said.

"Nice. I go Denver long time ago. What you say? High mile city?"

Blake grinned. "Mile high city."

Charlie threw his head back and laughed. "Yes, yes, yes. Mile high city. No high mile city." He shook his head. Everyone at the table laughed with him. Charlie was funny. "I bring you potstickers," he said as he backed away from the table, still laughing.

The potstickers were delicious, crispy and loaded with flavor. He served them with a sweet and tangy sauce.

"Can we just order more of these and skip the next stop?" Lydia asked.

"I hear that a lot," Jamal said. "But I think you'll like our next two stops."

They bowed to Charlie and thanked him as they left. "You come see Charlie next trip to Charlotte," he said.

Two blocks away, Lydia recognized her surroundings. "Cambri's condo is right there," she said, inclining her head toward the tall, brown brick building.

"And there's the roof where you read," Blake said, his dimple making an appearance and a twinkle in his eye.

"I can't believe I spent the entire summer that close to Charlie's, and today's the day I discover his potstickers. And they deliver," she said, poking fun at herself. Blake laughed, and thousands of Elmos started tickling her insides. It felt a little thrilling to be the one who made him smile.

Jamal pulled his Segway to a stop outside a restaurant called Globe and took off his helmet as the others pulled in beside him. When they were all parked and unhelmeted, he spoke. "This is Globe. It was opened just over a year ago, and you're only our second group to go here since they agreed to participate in our tour. Vito Cornelli is the executive chef." Lydia gasped, and her eyes lit up. "You know who he is?" Jamal asked Lydia.

"He was on Chef Wars."

"That's right. He was the runner up on the reality show Chef Wars. He's known for doing some crazy stuff with food. He'll feed you things you never thought you could eat. Don't worry." He laughed at the teenagers' expressions of concern. "For the tour, he keeps it pretty normal. We're eating a scallop and pasta dish." He laughed again at the teenage girl. "You're a picky one, aren't you? Is it the scallops?" She nodded. "He has chicken for anyone who's not into seafood."

Jamal led the way to the large table set up in the back of the room. Lydia recognized Vito Cornelli from the show. He looked more like a lineman for the Broncos than a chef. His head was completely hairless, except for his eyebrows and half inch strip of beard that started at his lower lip and ended at his chin. His chef's coat was rolled up to his elbows, and his thick arms were folded over his broad chest, his feet shoulder width apart. All they needed was a platform, some creepy lighting, and some smoke, and he could have been on Iron Chef.

He inclined his head. "Welcome. Any questions about your lunch?" he asked when they were all seated.

The teenage boy held up a finger and started to talk. "Since you're famous from your time on television, what would make you open a restaurant in Charlotte, instead of a larger market, say New York or Los Angeles?"

Vito glanced his direction then back at the entire table. "Any questions about your lunch?" he enunciated slowly. "As in *the food.*"

The teenage boy fell back in his seat, deflated. Lydia felt sorry for him, even though he'd been irritating the entire tour.

When no one dared ask a question, he turned to Jamal. "Scallops or chicken?"

"Scallops, baby!" Jamal said, trying to ease the tension.

Vito looked at the next person at the table with raised eyebrows. "Chicken," the teenage girl said timidly. Vito continued his eye-piercing trip around the table, and each person announced their preference. Then Vito left.

"I promise it'll be worth putting up with his ego," Jamal whispered. "He's won all kinds of awards and you'll see. His food is amazing."

Jamal was right. The scallop and pasta dish was buttery and garlicky and rich. The seasoned vegetables were almost as good as the pasta.

"I wonder if Globe delivers," Blake said and bumped Lydia's arm with his elbow.

"If Vito was the one to deliver it, I'd have been too scared to order. He's pretty intimidating."

"Was he that intense on the show?"

"He had a few debates with the judges. Especially the episode when he was eliminated."

"He'd have probably won if he'd served this," Blake said, soaking up the sauce on his plate with his last bite of bread."

Vito never reappeared, so when the food was gone, the tour slid out of their chairs and left.

The last stop was Liaison Amoureuse , a dessert café and bakery less than two blocks away. "Liaison Amoureuse is owned by a French pastry chef named Corinne Blanchet. You won't believe she's old enough to be a chef, let alone own her own business."

The inside of Liaison Amoureuse was beautiful. The décor was mostly creams and ivories. The wooden chairs at the tables were a deep plum, and plum pendant lights hung in uneven clusters above the tables. The walls were covered with love letters.

"Yay! You are here," said a tiny woman who nearly bounced out of the kitchen. Her almost-black hair was styled in a short, pixie cut. From a distance, she looked about twelve years old, but as she approached the group, she aged to somewhere in her thirties. "How has your tour been?"

They nodded and said things like, "Great," "so much fun," and "perfect."

"You're lucky to have Jamal. He's the best," she said with a gentle punch to Jamal's arm.

"She says that to all the guides."

"No, she doesn't," said the petite woman.

"This is Corinne Blanchet," Jamal said, and Corinne curtsied.

"And this is Liaison Amoureuse," said Corinne, opening her arms to take in the restaurant. Her accent made everything sound romantic. "In French, *liaison amoureuse* means love affair, and I want everyone who comes in here to have a love affair with dessert."

"Tell them about the love letters," Jamal said.

"My parents were moving to the south of France and they were tossing most of their souvenirs and I saw a trunk of their letters to each other. They were going to throw them away." She sounded incredulous. "I rescued them, and when I read them they were lovely. Some were a little hmm hmm," she said putting her hands on her cheeks and shaking her head. "They're up high so you can't read them. Scandalous!"

Lydia looked at the letters on the wall. There had to be over a hundred. "These are all from your parents?" she asked.

"No, no, no. Anyone who wants to bring me a nice copy of a love letter, I'll put it on the wall. I read them all before I put them up. They're so romantic, I fall in love with them. Please, come sit down." When they were all seated, Corinne continued, "I believe dessert is the most important meal of the day." Her enthusiasm was catching and everyone at the table smiled. "In honor of our beautiful city, dessert will be *Charlotte à la Framboise*. In English, that's a Charlotte cake with a raspberry filling. It will be served with two sauces, a raspberry and pear reduction, which is a more traditional sauce with a Charlotte, and a ganache, because some people, like me, just need chocolate with their dessert. Enjoy." She kissed her fingers and threw them into the air.

The Charlotte was incredible—buttery and crisp cake and moist, sweet filling. Blake preferred the raspberry and pear sauce, but Lydia couldn't get enough of the chocolate.

"Are Elliott's letters too sad to share?" Blake asked when his dessert was finished. Lydia still had several bites. She was eating it slowly, making it last as long as possible.

"Not the first ones," she said. "They were very romantic."

"We should make a copy and bring one in. Leave a piece of history here."

"That's a great idea. Francie said they were part of history," Lydia said. "Oh my. I've never tasted anything like this." She licked her fork after her last bite.

Blake was deep in thought as they rode their Segways back to the City Tours office. Lydia stifled her curiosity and left him to his thoughts. After they'd parked the Segways, returned the helmets, and said their thank yous and goodbyes to Jamal, they walked to their car. Blake unlocked Lydia's door but didn't open it.

"I was thinking I'd like to take the box back to Francie."

"Really?"

"I'm pretty sure I broke her heart yesterday. If we left now, do you think we'd have time to make copies for me and take the box back to Boone before our flight?"

"As long as our car doesn't break down," Lydia said.

"Let's do it."

Blake stepped back into City Tours and asked Jamal for directions, and twenty minutes later, they were in a copy and print store with the shoe box. Lydia took a letter out of the envelope and handed it to Blake, who made a copy and handed the original back to Lydia, who had the next letter ready to copy. They made a copy of each letter for Blake and an extra copy of the first one to send to Corinne at Liaison Amoureuse. It didn't take long. Blake tucked a folder with all the copies in his briefcase, and they took the Interstate north to Boone.

"Would you call Francie and see if she can meet us?" Blake asked and handed Lydia his phone. "It's the number that starts eight two eight."

"Should I tell her why we're coming?" Lydia asked.

"Sure." Lydia found the number and dialed it. On the third ring, Francie answered. "Hi, Francie. This is Lydia. I came with Blake yesterday. We're on our way to Boone right now and wanted to meet you. Will you be home in the next couple hours?"

"I can be. Was there something else you needed?"

"Blake made copies of the letters for himself, and he wants you to have the box. We'll just swing by your house as soon as we get to town."

Francie took a deep breath before she replied. "I'll be here. Thank you."

"I think she might have been crying," Lydia said. Blake looked at her and smiled. "This is very thoughtful of you."

"I got what Grandpa wanted me to get out of it. I think it means a lot to her. She should have it."

Lydia was still holding Blake's phone when it rang. She turned it over and looked at the screen. "It's Brynn." She handed it to Blake.

Twelve

lake didn't want to answer the phone. His calls with Brynn and Mary Challis this morning hadn't been entirely productive. Brynn was being unreasonable, and Mary was being high maintenance. Sure, it would have been better if he was there in the office holding her hand through the whole thing, but she was an adult. She'd survive until tomorrow morning. And Brynn. She'd taken a two-week vacation to Hawaii in April. Did she really think Blake didn't deserve a few days away from the office to take care of a personal matter?

"Hi, Brynn." It was work to keep his voice patient and upbeat.

"Blake, Mr. Van Wagoner wants to speak to you. I'm putting you through to him."

Fantastic. He'd hoped to have everything resolved without any of the partners having to be involved.

"Blake, my man. Is it true you're in North Carolina?" His tone was falsely chipper, and it grated on Blake.

"It's true. I came out over the weekend for a family matter, and my flight was cancelled on Sunday."

"And here it is Tuesday. They really need to schedule more flights between North Carolina and Denver." He paused, waiting for a response from Blake, but he waited in vain. Blake didn't feel like explaining anything else. He refused to kowtow any more than necessary in front of Lydia. "When can we expect you back?"

"I'm on a flight this evening. I'm meeting with Mary Challis in the morning."

"About that meeting. I just got off the phone with David Austin's attorney a few minutes ago. He received a call from a rather upset Mary Challis, demanding to know why he thought he deserved two percent of her share. He wants this wrapped up and her put on a leash."

"I've spoken with her. She's upset, but we're going to work it out tomorrow morning."

"This takeover—"

"Merger, sir," Blake interrupted.

Pryce Van Wagoner sighed. "We all know it's a merger, Blake, but the fact is, Mr. Austin's side is bringing a lot more money to the table, and when it's all finished, Mary will be involved only inasmuch as she'll have a large stockholding. She won't be involved in the day-to-day operations." He was talking to Blake like he was a first-year law student. "And let's not forget this deal stands to make the firm a tidy profit."

Blake wanted to protest, to remind Mr. Van Wagoner that their firm represented Mary Challis and that it was Blake's job to be sure she was treated fairly, even if it meant the deal fell through. But Blake knew if he wanted to be a partner, picking a fight with Pryce would probably be a costly error. "I understand. I think it's a good deal for her, and once I meet with her, I think she'll see the advantage of moving forward and not getting bogged down by a couple of percentage points."

"Good. I'll let Mr. Austin's lawyer know you're on the case."

"Thank you, Mr. Van Wagoner."

"I've told you to call me Pryce."

"Thank you, Pryce."

"And Blake, you be sure that airline knows we need you bright and early tomorrow morning. No more cancelled flights. And how about once you're here, no more flights, period, for the next decade." There was a long pause. "Just kidding, just kidding." He sounded phony. "Have a nice trip home."

"I'll see you tomorrow," Blake said. He turned off the phone, resisting the urge to throw it out the window. He put it in the tray between the seats then massaged the bridge of his nose.

Lydia didn't interrupt his thoughts, and finally he said, "I may have blown any chance at partner."

"I'm sure you'll be fine. You'll get everything straightened out."

Blake shook his head. "They're not too happy with me right now."

"They will be once you're home and you make the sale," Lydia said. Blake chuckled and smiled. "I said that wrong, didn't I?"

"Mr. Van Wagoner would be very offended if he knew you thought of him as a salesman."

"Then I'm glad he didn't hear me. I suppose if I'm going to give you a pep talk, I guess I should know a little more what I'm talking about."

"What you said was perfect. Seriously."

The rest of the drive to Boone was mostly quiet. Lydia even dozed off for a little while at the end, which gave Blake time to think. How was he supposed to follow Grandpa's advice when people like Mr. Van Wagoner had his future in their hands? Blake wondered if Pryce had put in eighty hour weeks when he'd started his career. He probably had. Maybe that explained the two ex-Mrs. Van Wagoners.

Francie must have been waiting for them just inside the door because she answered before they were even through knocking. "Please, come in."

"I could tell these were really important to you, so I want you to have them," Blake said when they were inside the front door. "Thank you for letting me take them."

"But your grandfather wanted you to have them. Of course I want them back, but I don't know if I feel right taking them when he and Grandma had already made arrangements."

"Grandpa wanted me to know what was in them, and I do now. He'd be fine with me giving them back to you. There is one thing, though."

"What's that?" Francie looked suspicious.

"If you don't mind, I'd really love to have the Celtics tickets. Grandpa was a huge Celtics fan, and he took my Dad to see them whenever they played the Nuggets. I know it would mean a lot to my dad to have those."

"Oh, of course." Francie placed the box on the entryway table and searched through the contents until she had them. "Are you sure there's nothing else in here you want? Maybe one of the letters?"

"I have a letter he wrote to me before he died and copies of these. That's all I need. Thank you again for letting me take them."

"Thank you for bringing them back." Francie patted her heart. "I'm very grateful."

Blake felt more at peace than he had in a long time. He spent so much of his time with tasks that held little reward. But this—this felt right.

"We'd better hurry," he said when they were back in the car. "I really can't miss this flight."

Thirteen

The drive to the airport and the wait by the gate was pleasant enough, but Blake seemed preoccupied. Lydia wondered if he regretted returning the letters to Francie or if it was the impending problems he had to deal with at work. Whatever it was, he seemed further away.

"Are you as tired as I am?" he asked when they were sitting beside each other on the plane.

"I'm pretty tired," Lydia answered. She wondered if this was Blake's way to politely go to sleep and eliminate the need for conversation.

It had seemed like they had a real connection the past few days, and Lydia hoped they'd see each other when they got back to Denver. She'd joked with Cambri about having a little summer fling. Could she count this as her fling when she reported back? It didn't feel like a fling. It felt like much more and much less than a fling. More because it didn't feel flingy. It felt real and special and important. Hadn't they shared more than they would have if it were just a fling? But sadly, it was also less than a fling. They hadn't held hands. Not really. And they hadn't kissed. Could a summer fling really be a fling without a kiss? And could she think the word "fling" one more time and still take herself seriously?

Maybe when they reached Denver, she should take this little bit of bravery she'd shown over the last few days, multiply it by a thousand, and *fling* her arms around his neck and give him a kiss he wouldn't forget. At least then she could technically count this as a real summer romance.

She sighed.

"You okay?" Blake asked.

"I'm fine. Just tired."

"You can sleep on my shoulder if it's more comfortable."

It was such a sweet gesture that of course she had to take him up on the offer. You don't have a man who looks like Blake offer his shoulder and say no. "Thanks. I think I will." She shifted in her seat and leaned her head against his shoulder, but there was nowhere to put her arm. If she put it on the armrest, it put her at an awkward angle. If she put it right by her side, it was wedged between her body and the armrest, and it was painful.

"Here." Blake took her arm and looped it through his. Her hand now rested on his arm. His other hand rested on hers. "Better?"

"Much better." *Please don't let this be just a fling.*

Even though she was tired, Lydia was sure she wouldn't be able to fall asleep. Not with Blake's hand sending shivers up her arm. Not with her cheek resting on his warm, strong shoulder.

And then she woke up. She lifted her head and looked around. The cabin was dark except for a few lights where passengers must have been reading.

"We'll be landing in about ten minutes," Blake said. Lydia was too embarrassed to snuggle back into his shoulder, so she leaned her head back on the seat, glad her arm was still linked through his.

"Did you sleep at all?" she asked softly.

"A little."

They sat in silence after that. Lydia tried to give herself a motivational speech. *Really brave girls aren't afraid to initiate a kiss. Just stand on your tiptoes and kiss him. Or maybe it would be more romantic to put her hand behind his neck and pull him down to her.* A kiss would be the perfect ending to the last three days, and it would definitely salvage her lamentable summer. And maybe, if it was a really good kiss, it wouldn't be an ending at all. Maybe it would be the beginning . . .

Don't go there. Just think about the kiss.

The plane landed and the lights came on. The fasten seatbelt sign switched off with a bell, and Lydia reluctantly let go of Blake's arm. The rows ahead of them disembarked, and finally it was their turn to go. Blake handed Lydia her carryon and pulled down his duffle bag. She followed him off the plane, silently cheering herself on all the way. When the portable walkway opened into the terminal, Blake slowed down to walk beside her. "My car's in the long-term parking. Do you need a ride?"

"My brother's fiancé is probably already here," she said. "Thanks anyway." *Kiss him.*

"I'll walk down with you to get your bags and help you get them to her car. That's a lot for one person to try to manage."

"Thanks. That'd be great." *You can do it. Kiss him.*

They stood by the carousel and waited. *Just do it. Kiss him. Kiss him. Kiss him.*

When they'd collected the bags, they walked out to the sidewalk. There was Cambri, waving to be sure Lydia had seen her. Lydia waved back. *You're such a chicken. If you wouldn't do it before, you won't do it with Cambri watching.*

Cambri squealed and pulled Lydia into a hug, then stepped back to look at her. "This summer's been good for you. You look great." Lydia looked at Blake, and they both burst out laughing. "What? Did I miss something?"

"I'll tell you all about it in the car," Lydia said. "This is Blake. Blake, this is Cambri."

They shook hands, then Cambri discreetly got in the car. *This is your chance. Kiss him.*

And then as her mind told her to kiss him, her hand betrayed her and she reached out to shake his hand. Blake looked surprised but he put out his hand and shook hers. "Thanks, Blake. I had a nice time."

"Me too. Thanks for all your help."

Then she got in the car. Lydia turned to look at Blake as Cambri signaled to pull out. He was standing there watching her, his duffle bag over his shoulder. She waved, and his look of confusion changed into a smile. Cambri pulled into traffic, and a moment later, Blake was gone.

"Who was that?" Cambri asked.

"I'm so stupid. 'I had a nice time?' Really? That's what you'd say at the end of a boring date with someone you never want to see again. Not at the end of the most amazing three days of your life to someone who saved your summer and who you committed a crime for." Lydia threw her head back against the seat.

"Whoa. Start again. I'm completely lost. What just happened?"

Lydia spent the entire drive home telling Cambri every detail of the last three days. It wasn't until she was home that she realized she hadn't told her anything about the three months before Sunday.

Fourteen

What had just happened? Blake stood on the sidewalk watching Lydia's friend's car leave the airport. Lydia had turned toward him, her face illuminated by the bright lights that lined the drop off and pick up area. She'd had the same look on her face that she'd had that first day when she'd told him about her failed summer. And then she'd waved. Blake waved back and smiled. She was like a bird, skittish and jumpy until she psyched herself up. He'd seen it that first day and the day of their sky dive.

Blake was disappointed. The entire flight home, he'd resisted the temptation to kiss the top of her head. He'd been wanting to kiss her since she leaped into his arms after they'd jumped, but he hadn't wanted to scare her away. All the way home, he'd planned to pull her into a hug and kiss her goodbye at the airport.

And then she'd stuck out her hand. He should have used that hand to pull her into the hug. Or teased her and said something clever. Instead, he'd shaken her hand and said "Thanks for your help." Thanks for your help? The last three days had been thrilling and emotional and funny and sweet. And he'd just said 'thanks for your help.'"

It was after ten when Blake unlocked the door to his apartment. He'd turned the air conditioning down when he'd left, and the room felt too warm and stuffy. The difference between Charlotte and Denver was that in Charlotte, even the air outside was hot and muggy. In Denver, the night air was cool and refreshing and all Blake had to do was open the windows. One advantage of living in the high mile city. Blake smiled as he thought of Charlie. He couldn't think about Charlie without thinking about Lydia and how much she'd enjoyed Charlie and those potstickers. She'd enjoyed everything.

Lydia hadn't cowered in the corner of the plane refusing to jump. She'd willingly learned how to Segway. She'd taken a risk when it was needed at Shady Days. She wasn't a coward at all. Somehow, she'd convinced herself she was a boring and unadventurous person, but she was wrong. He should have told her.

He would tell her. After they'd been home for a few days, and she was settled into the new school year and after the Challis-Austin deal was finalized, he'd tell her. He'd call her and they'd go out to dinner and he'd tell her how brave she was and how beautiful she was and how much he liked her. Maybe they'd skip dinner and go rock climbing or skiing. Maybe she'd want to go to a Nuggets game with him. There were so many things he wanted to do with her.

Blake didn't even unpack. He plugged his phone in to charge and went to bed thinking of adventures he'd like to share with Lydia.

Fifteen

The teacher's meeting lasted two weeks. At least that's how it felt. Mrs. Gentry, the principal, had a high-pitched, sing-song voice that hummed on and on. How much of her summer had been spent figuring out different ways to say "The kids are our top priority?"

"The kids are our top priority." "We have to put the kids first." "We do this for the kids." Blah, blah, blah. "These kids need to know they're number one." Blah, blah, blah. "These kids mean more to us than life itself." Okay, she didn't really say that one, but she might as well have.

Lydia relived the curb at the airport while Mrs. Gentry babbled on and on, only this time, she daydreamed about the way she wished she'd have handled it. She'd come up with three romantic scenarios when Cate Espinosa jabbed her in the arm and whispered, "At least try to *look* like you're paying attention."

"Yikes. That noticeable?" Lydia whispered back.

"Yeah. Someone's not ready for school to start." Lydia smiled and did her best to focus on what Mrs. Gentry was saying. It wasn't easy.

During the afternoon session, the school counselor, a nurse and a member of the school board addressed them. The counselor was pretty interesting, but fevers and head lice just couldn't keep her attention, so Lydia started writing a list of things to do on the first day of school, but soon the list had turned into Blake's name in all kinds of script.

Lydia was hopeless. The last three days had spoiled her. A life of skydiving and Segwaying and treasure hunting wasn't realistic, and a shy, small-town school teacher had about as much chance with Ryan Gosling as an orange had of becoming the main ingredient in banana bread. She scribbled through Blake's name. It was time to focus.

At four o'clock, the meetings finally ended. Lydia hadn't had a chance to get a few things she needed for her bulletin boards, so she made a quick trip to the craft store and the drive through for a sandwich. It was going to be a long evening, but she didn't mind.

Cambri called just as she arrived back at the school. "How you holding up? You must be pretty tired today."

"Tired wasn't my problem. I couldn't focus at all. I just kept thinking about Blake."

"Have you heard from him?"

"No. He's got such a stressful job, and he's behind and he wants to make partner. He'll be putting in a lot of long days. And after our goodbye last night . . ." Lydia sighed.

"Yeah, that was unfortunate."

"I don't know what's wrong with me. It's like my mind and my body aren't connected or my subconscious is so afraid I'll make a fool of myself that I end up making a fool of myself. I'm sure he thinks I'm not interested."

"So set him straight." Lydia laughed. "Seriously Lyd, call him. Tell him you like him. Tell him you want to see him again. What could it hurt?"

"My pride."

"Who cares about pride when true love is a possibility?"

Cambri said it like she was Scarlett O'Hara, and Lydia could picture her raising her wrist to her forehead dramatically.

"I've got to get busy, or I'll be here all night."

"All right. But listen. Your summer was supposed to be about adventure and bravery, and this guy helped you reach your goals. I think you should finish off your summer with one more tiny act of bravery. I think you should call him. You don't have to tell him you want to marry him and have a dozen little Blakies. Just say you'd like to get together sometime."

"Oh Cambri, I don't know. I want to be brave, but . . ."

"I remember a friend coming and picking me up to go for a drive and dropping me off at Jace's. And then you left me there. Is that what I need to do? Come pick you up and drop you off at Blake's?"

"I only did that because you're both so stubborn."

"And thank goodness you did. But Lydia, there's no harm in letting this guy know you're interested. If he is too, he's close enough for you guys to see each other. If he's not, he's far enough away that you're not going to run into each other in Bridger or Fort Collins."

"That's true. I'll think about it."

"Good girl. Now go get those bulletin boards done."

Lydia thought about what Cambri had said as she finished her sandwich. It was true. What did she have to lose? If he wasn't interested, this would just be an ego boost for him. If he was interested, they could . . .

Stop! Lydia was not going to get ahead of herself. That would only cause disappointment when it didn't happen. *Stay grounded.* Right now it was about being brave, and you couldn't be brave in the future. You could only be brave in the moment.

Sixteen

lake got to the office a little before seven in the morning. He had a few things to get ready before Mary Challis arrived at eight-thirty, and it wouldn't hurt to have Mr. Van Wagoner come in and see Blake already hard at work.

Brynn stopped by his door an hour later. "Good idea beating Pryce here. Maybe this will help him forget how badly you screwed up."

Blake tried not to show his annoyance. "Thanks for helping me out while I was gone. It was good to finally get the box my grandpa left me." Not that anyone at the office had cared.

It was hard not to be a little bitter. Brynn had worked with him ever since he'd come to Collins, Strider and Van Wagoner. He'd thought they were friends. He'd thought Finn and Andy were his friends. They'd been working hard for the past two years just like him. But no one here had asked how he was when his grandpa died. No one had cared that it was important to him to get the box. These people weren't really friends. They were associates. His life was filled with clients and associates. He'd been taking all his time away from people who mattered and giving it to people who knew nothing about him. This was what Grandpa had been talking about. Permanent and temporary. He got it.

"I'd better get to work," Blake said, turning his attention back to the files on his desk.

Pryce Van Wagoner walked through ten minutes later. Blake would have missed him entirely if he hadn't looked up at that moment. But he did, and he watched Pryce walk by the glass wall of his office. There was no reaction, no inclination of the head in greeting, no hello. It was just a glance in Blake's direction.

Mary Challis arrived a few minutes early, but Blake was ready for her. He met her at the door and shook her damp hand. She sat on the edge of her seat and fidgeted. "I'm sorry I spoiled your vacation, Mr. Knowles. I've just been so worried. Hank took care of everything like this when he was alive, and I'm just so afraid I'm going to make a mistake."

"I don't think you're making a mistake. We'll go through all the numbers together, and I think you'll see this is a good deal for you. If you don't, we'll walk away and you can take another route. We want you to be happy with the deal."

Mary visibly relaxed. "I hope I didn't get you in trouble. Your boss was pretty upset when I talked to him."

"Nah, everything here's fine."

Blake picked up the files and took the seat beside Mary. For the next two hours they went over the numbers. He explained how much she'd get up front and what her expected return would be at thirty-three percent and at thirty-five percent. "So you can see, this is still a good number," Blake said. "I'm not sure risking a sure thing for only a little more would be worth it. If we back out, it might take a long time to find another deal, and you'll have to pay overhead and expenses that whole time. It could end up being more expensive to wait than to take this."

Mary sighed. "I don't want to try to run things anymore. I don't know enough to feel confident I'm doing things right, and every night I go to bed worrying I'm going to ruin Hank's company."

"It's your company now. But if you take the deal, you'll still get almost a third of the profits in addition to the cash up front, and you can stop worrying about the day-to-day operations." He pointed at the number on the paper. "If you don't buy a small island in the Caribbean, you can live pretty comfortably on the up-front money, and the thirty-three percent will just be extra every quarter."

"Thank you, Blake," Mary Challis said as she was leaving. "You've been very patient and helpful."

After she was gone, Blake got busy on the stack of work that had piled up while he was gone. It was daunting. Had they purposely added extra to the workload so he'd never leave them hanging again, or did this really represent what he'd have done if he'd been there? He wasn't sure.

Blake's mind kept wandering to Lydia. Was she sitting in her meeting right now? Where would she eat lunch? If she had a sandwich, would she ask them to go light on the mayo? What would she tell her class about skydiving? If he'd kissed her, would she have kissed him back? Had she thought about him at all?

Just before five, Brynn stuck her head in the door. "I'm getting the guys Mexican tonight. Any requests?"

This was the way they always did things. "The guys" were actually three men and two women, including Blake. Almost every evening, the staff and the partners headed home at a reasonable time. Brynn's last duty of the day was to pick up dinner and bring it back for the underlings who would work until bedtime. They'd get together for twenty minutes and eat in the break room, then they'd get back to work. This was the price that had to be paid to impress the partners. If you were one of the lucky ones who eventually made partner, you could look forward to eating dinner with your family or heading to the gym while the inferiors worked themselves to death to impress you.

It was madness. Blake thought of Grandpa's letter, and suddenly he wanted to see Lydia. He wanted to read it with her. He should have shared it with her in North Carolina, but it had felt like he'd be exposing too much. He'd have been too vulnerable.

Lydia's face flashed into his mind. Not her face when she was skydiving or walking out of Janet's office with a look of triumph. It wasn't her face as she enjoyed the potstickers at Charlie's. It was the face in the window of her friend's car as she was leaving. Suddenly, Blake understood her expression. He knew why she'd stuck her hand out awkwardly. She was feeling vulnerable, too. She'd been protecting herself.

It was time for him to do something brave. He'd share the letter and tell her how he felt. If he were a betting man, he'd wager she felt the same way, but if she didn't, that was okay. At least he wouldn't spend his life wondering if this was a girl he could have had a future with.

"Uh, Blake." Brynn made his name into two syllables. "I asked if you had any requests?"

"No. I'm going to head out in just a few minutes." Blake knew what he was doing was going to cost him, and he felt a little sick inside.

Brynn folded her arms, and her face turned hard. "You're kidding."

"No, I've got some things I need to do tonight. Thanks anyway."

Brynn stood in the doorway, watching him for what felt like a very long time. Blake could see her out of the corner of his eye, but he didn't make eye contact. He just kept working until finally, finally she left.

At a little after five-thirty, Blake closed his office door and walked past the break room. He could hear the guys in there joking and having dinner. The bell on the elevator rang as Alice Strider, one of the partners, walked up beside him. Her face held a question, but they rode the elevator to the parking garage in silence.

Seventeen

ydia stapled a large piece of blue butcher paper to the first bulletin board. At the bottom of the board she planned to put the top half of a cartoon child's face, the large eyes looking up. Above his head in the sky would be thought bubbles with inspirational quotes. She'd printed off the child's face and the quotes last spring when she'd searched for classroom ideas on Pinterest. She pulled a large manila folder that held the printed pieces from a filing cabinet in the corner behind her desk.

The filing cabinet reminded her of Janet's office, and she thought about Blake. What would he be doing right now? He probably had so much work to catch up that he'd be at the office late into the evening. Maybe he was eating a sandwich at his desk. He might not have time to take a phone call even if she did get up the courage.

She took the half face and stapled it on top of the blue butcher paper. It was a cute cartoon face with electric blue eyes. Hmm. Who else had eyes that color? Lydia shook her head. What was she? Fourteen?

Lydia unfolded the first thought bubble and stapled it above the face. It read, "All our dreams can come true if we have the courage to pursue them. Walt Disney."

The second bubble said, "Creativity takes courage. Henri Matisse."

The third made Lydia smile. She must have been thinking of her summer in Charlotte when she was preparing this bulletin board. "Life shrinks or expands in proportion to one's courage. Anaïs Nin."

That was certainly true. The entire summer seemed small and anemic, while the last three days of her trip had been robust and bursting with feelings and energy and emotions. Her life had expanded when she'd decided to take a chance and do something adventurous.

She thought about Blake—his smile, his dimple, but mostly, his thoughtfulness. She'd stayed in Charlotte those two extra days to help him find the box, and even though that was their goal, he'd arranged the skydiving and the Segway tour. He hadn't selfishly made the days all about him. He'd thought of her. When he'd seen Francie suffering because of the loss of her grandmother's belongings, he'd arranged to return them to her.

There were qualities more important than absurdly good looks or the ability to stir the hummingbirds in her stomach into a reckless fit. She'd witnessed his love for his grandfather, his patience with clients and coworkers, as well as his kindness and generosity.

She had to do something. She was a senseless coward if she didn't let Blake know how she felt.

Lydia stepped off the stool and retrieved her cell phone from her purse. She sat down at her desk and looked at the Walt Disney thought bubble again. "All our dreams can come true if we have the courage to pursue them." Maybe Walt knew what he was talking about. Lydia pulled up Blake's number, pressed the talk button, and held the phone to her ear.

Her stomach was folding in on itself, and she felt oddly winded.

After a moment, the call connected and Lydia heard the first ring in her ear. Three seconds later it rang again. Strange. It sounded louder. Another three seconds, and she heard it ring in her ear . . . and outside her door. It didn't ring a fourth time.

"Hello," Blake said. He was standing in the doorway, holding his phone to his ear.

Lydia stood up from her desk so quickly, her chair slid into the wall behind her. She pushed the end button on her phone and slowly lowered it from her ear.

"Hi Lydia. Did I just miss a call from you?" Blake said.

If breathing had been difficult before the phone call, it was nearly impossible now. *Breathe. You don't want to pass out and miss this moment.* "What are you doing here?" Lydia asked.

"I came to see if you need any help getting your room ready for school." Blake stuck his phone in his pocket.

"You did?"

"Yes. But that wasn't the only reason I came. I really wanted to see you."

"Really?" *What an idiotic thing to say. You'd think someone who had read dozens of romances would be able to come up with something clever or flirty to say.*

Blake smiled. "Really."

"What about work?"

"Work will be there tomorrow."

Lydia put her hand to her heart to try to calm its frenzied hammering.

"You were calling me. Did you need something?"

Lydia took a deep breath. It was still scary to tell him how she felt, but he'd just made it easier. He'd just left work, driven to Fort Collins, found her school and even found her classroom. "How did you find my classroom?"

Blake laughed. "That's not what you were calling me about, but I passed a teacher by the front doors. He told me where you were." Blake stepped up to Lydia's desk. "You were calling?"

Be brave. Don't blow it again. Lydia stepped around the desk, and Blake turned to face her. "I just had something I wanted to tell you," she said.

"Okay." Blake sat down on the edge of her desk and folded his arms in front of him. "Should I be nervous?"

"Maybe. I know I am." Lydia shoved her hands into her pockets and bit her bottom lip, taking a moment to give herself a little internal pep talk. "I've been beating myself up for the way I said goodbye yesterday. Blake, I didn't want to shake your hand."

"You didn't?" Blake's mouth quirked up at the side.

"No. I wanted to be brave."

"What would the brave Lydia have done?" His voice was teasing, and suddenly Lydia wasn't nervous at all.

"She'd have done this." The atmosphere wasn't perfect. The fluorescent lights were too bright, a vacuum cleaner or floor polisher was humming from somewhere down the hall, and her hair was up in a high, messy ponytail. But Lydia didn't care. Blake was here and that was all that really mattered.

When she'd pictured this moment in her mind, she'd had to stand on her tiptoes, but with Blake leaning on her desk, they were almost exactly the same height. Lydia moved closer and gently pressed her lips to Blake's, briefly at first, but then again, a little longer. He leaned toward her as she pulled away, prolonging the kiss.

"That's what I wanted to do at the airport," she said softly. "But I was too afraid."

Blake's arm circled Lydia's waist and pulled her close. "And this is what I wanted to do at the airport," he said. His arm held her against him as his free hand came up and pulled her to his lips, his thumb on her jaw and his fingers on the nape of her neck. The kiss was long and slow and soft as his thumb moved along her jaw before he moved his hand to her waist. Lydia put her arms around his neck and touched the soft hair at his collar. His lips moved against hers until they were both breathless and in need of air. "This is much better than shaking hands," he whispered in her ear and then nuzzled into her neck.

Lydia didn't want to move. If a genie had granted her one wish in that moment, it would have been that they could stay here, suspended in time, his warm arms forever around her, his cheek touching hers, his breath on her neck.

"So now I know why you were calling me," he said, not letting her go. "But I need to tell you why I came to see you." Lydia pulled back and looked into his eyes. "I want to share my grandpa's letter with you."

"The one he wrote you?"

"Yes. I should have shared it with you in Charlotte, but I didn't know what it would say, and after the letters we'd read . . . Well, I was afraid it might say something that would scare you away." Lydia touched Blake's cheek softly. "But when I thought about you today, I knew I wanted you to hear it."

Lydia leaned forward and kissed him again. "Do you have it with you?" She asked between kisses.

He rested his forehead against hers. "It's in my car. Let's finish what you need to do in here then we'll go somewhere and read it."

It was difficult to concentrate on work with Blake's warm arms and soft lips so close, but they managed to finish the two bulletin boards and organize the bookshelf. All Lydia had left to do was assemble the beginning-of-the-year papers for the parents, but that could wait until tomorrow. Less than an hour later, Lydia turned off the light and they walked out of the school holding hands.

Eighteen

The sun had slipped behind the mountains in the distance, leaving the peaks silhouetted against the dark, purple sky. They left Lydia's car in the parking lot and drove to Cicero's Pizza where they sat kitty-corner at a table in the back and ordered a pizza. Blake had brought the letter in, and as soon as they'd placed their order, he took it out of the envelope.

Lydia turned toward him, her chin in her hand. Blake wanted to kiss her again. He would after he read her the letter. He unfolded the pages then reached down and held her hand in her lap and started quietly reading.

Blake read the entire letter before he looked up. When he'd finished, he pulled his hand away long enough to fold it and put it back in the envelope. He reached for her hand again.

"Thank you for sharing that with me," Lydia said. Blake gave a short nod. "It isn't scaring me away." How did she know he needed to hear those words? Lydia pulled him close and kissed his dimple. His breath caught and he turned to brush her lips with his.

He looked down at her hands and played with her fingers. "I left work today because I've made some decisions. I don't know what's going to happen with my job. I know that if I follow Grandpa's advice, I'll never become a partner at Collins, Strider and Van Wagoner, and I don't know if they'll even want me there if I'm not willing to put in those hours. And I know it's too soon for us to know what will happen here." He waved his hand back and forth between them. "But I know I want to find out." He pulled her hand up to his lips and kissed her fingers.

They ate pizza and talked about Blake's meeting with Mary Challis. Lydia told Blake about her meetings and her lack of concentration.

When the pizza was gone, Blake drove Lydia back to the empty parking lot at Juniper Heights Elementary. At the door of her car, he took her in his arms again and held her close, kissing her again. "I wish I could have met your grandpa," Lydia said. "I'd like to tell him thanks for sending you on that little treasure hunt."

"He'd feel pretty smug if he knew he was responsible for me meeting you."

"Maybe he does know," Lydia said.

"I hope he does." Blake held her door open, and Lydia got in her car. He leaned in and kissed her goodbye. "I'll see you tomorrow," he said as he closed the door.

Nineteen

Six Months Later

"Knock, knock." Lydia pushed open the door of the small house on Lincoln Street.

"Hey Lydia, come on in." Blake's new partner, Paul, was sitting on the floor, his back against the wall, looking at something on his cell phone. "Blake stopped by the management company's office to get the paperwork. He should be here any minute."

Lydia looked around the room. "This looks nice. Wasn't this an accounting firm before?"

"Yeah, they moved to a bigger place downtown."

Lydia wandered around, giving herself a tour. The interior didn't look like a house anymore. The entry was wide and open enough to make a comfortable waiting room with a reception desk. Off to one side was a large office that looked out at the street. A doorway at the back of the room led to another spacious office. A narrow hallway led to restrooms and a small kitchen.

"What do you think?" Blake asked, peeking his head through the kitchen door.

Lydia smiled. "It's perfect."

"I thought you'd like it." He placed a file folder on the counter and took her in his arms. Her fingers slid behind his neck, and she pulled him down and kissed him. "Mmm," he said against her lips. "I've missed you."

"I hope so. It's been two whole days."

"All right, you two. We've got paperwork to sign," Paul said, coming into the kitchen. Blake stepped back but put his arm around her shoulder.

"Did Jemma come with you?" Lydia asked.

"She's not feeling very well. Whoever called it morning sickness got it all wrong. She's pretty sick all day." Jemma was four months pregnant with their first baby.

"Tell her I hope she feels better."

"Thanks. I will."

Lydia turned back to Blake. "This definitely gets my stamp of approval."

"Good," Blake said. "Now that you and Jemma have both signed off on it, we can make it official."

"I'll leave you guys to the paperwork," said Lydia. "I'm going to run over to the school and grade some papers."

"I'll come get you when we're finished." Blake kissed her forehead.

The school was less than three miles from what would soon be Hansen and Knowles, Attorneys at Law. Lydia liked the proximity. She also liked Paul and Jemma.

Blake had been disappointed, but not surprised when Pryce had named Andy as the new partner, but just three weeks later, Blake had run into Paul at an alumni reception. They'd taken a few classes together in law school, and before the evening was over, they were making plans to open a small firm in Fort Collins.

Lydia graded essays on the Revolutionary War until her phone rang. "Hey, Lyd. I'm locked out of the school."

"I'll be right out."

Lydia couldn't help smiling when she saw Blake leaning against his car. He looked so good in a gray stocking cap and navy wool coat. When he pushed himself off the car and walked toward her, her insides melted.

He put his hands on her shoulders and kissed her. "Do you feel like taking a little walk?"

"Here?"

"Why not?" He smiled. It was so hard to know where to look when he smiled. Did she focus on his twinkling blue eyes? Or the crinkles at the side of them? But how could she ignore that little dimple? It practically begged for her undivided attention.

Lydia buttoned her coat, and Blake tied her scarf around her neck before taking her hand in his and slipping them into his pocket.

For a few blocks, they walked and talked about the office, Paul and Jemma, and a Revolutionary War essay that lamented the loss of lives all because of fancy tea.

The streetlights flickered to life as the sun slipped behind the mountains. The temperature dropped, and Lydia adjusted her scarf to cover part of her cold face.

"You're freezing. Maybe I should have driven you here."

"Driven me where?" Lydia asked, looking around the neighborhood.

Blake stopped walking and took her cold face in his hands and kissed her. His lips were surprisingly warm.

"Here," Blake said and turned her toward a red brick rambler with a realtor's sign in the front yard. "I looked at this today and I really like it. It needs a little sprucing up, but I thought maybe Jace could help me with that."

"It looks nice," Lydia said. "I didn't know you were looking at houses."

"I wasn't." Blake pulled her in front of him so they were both facing the house, his arms around her waist. Lydia crossed her arms over his and held his hands. "But then I started thinking how silly it would be to get a condo only to have to move again when we needed more room."

Lydia stopped breathing.

"This has three bedrooms, and it's close to the school and my new office. It doesn't have to be this one if you don't like it, but I was thinking we should get a house." He kissed her temple. "I'll move into it now, then this summer, when we get married, there'll be plenty of room for both of us. And eventually, for a family." His cheek rested against hers. It felt so nice she didn't want to move, but everything he'd said deserved a response.

She turned in his arms and held the sides of his coat in her fists. She grinned up at him. "You're assuming a lot, aren't you?"

"Just hoping you love me as much as I love you, 'cause I've pretty much planned out my entire life, and you're in every day of it."

Lydia stood on her tiptoes and pulled Blake closer. He put his arms around her back and covered her mouth with his. His lips moved against hers, warm and intense. When he started to pull away, she moved her hands up to his cheeks and kissed him again before moving to kiss his dimple and his jaw.

"I love you, too, Blake Knowles." She kissed him again.

"Whew!" Blake took a step back, reached in the breast pocket of his coat, and pulled out a tiny, silk bag. He opened the top and tipped the bag over into his hand. "I was hoping Francie hadn't sent this to me for nothing."

"Is that really—" Lydia took his outstretched hand in both of hers and looked at the familiar ring. "Oh, Blake."

"I know it's not that fancy, but I figured later—"

Lydia put her finger to Blake's lips. "Stop. Don't say another word. This ring couldn't be more perfect." Blake grabbed her hand as her finger left his lips, kissed it, then held it against his heart for a moment before he let it go. He took the ring and slipped it on her finger.

"I love it," Lydia whispered, and he wrapped her in his arms.

When she shivered, Blake took her hand, tucked it back into his pocket, and they started the walk back to the car.

"Know what I think?" Lydia said.

"What?"

"That this is going to be the best adventure of all," Lydia said.

Continue on for a sneak peak of Book 5 (Francie's story) in the Ripple Effect Series.

Author's Note

Dear Reader,

I'm humbled that you chose my book and hope you found reading it to be an enjoyable experience. I love to hear from readers, either directly on my Facebook author page, by email (kareylwhite@gmail.com) or through reviews on Goodreads and Amazon. (Yes, I read them.)

Getting a book noticed is a challenge, so if you're enjoying The Ripple Effect Romance series, please spread the word with your reading friends.

Thank you and Happy Reading!
Karey

Acknowledgements

Thanks to Rachael and Kaylee for the opportunity to do this together and for sharing my philosophy about writing. Thank you to Julie, Donna and Jennifer for enthusiastically joining the party.

Thank you to my first readers—Rachael, Kaylee, Savannah and Mom (Karen). Your enthusiasm and input were very helpful.

Thank you to my family, whose support and encouragement make it possible for me to do this.

Finally, thank you to all of you who read what I write. I'm very blessed.

About Karey White

Karey is a *USA Today* bestselling author. She grew up in Utah, Idaho, Oregon, and Missouri. She attended Ricks College and Brigham Young University. Her first novel, *Gifted*, was a Whitney Award Finalist.

She loves to travel, read, cook, and spend time with family and friends. She and her husband are the parents of four wonderful children.

Find out more about Karey at KareyWhite.com.

Coming next in the Ripple Effect Romance Series
(Available May 5, 2014)

Thirty-seven year old Francie Davis, a recent widow and empty nester, gets to attend college at last. She's sure her luck has changed when she also lands a job on campus that will pay her tuition, as administrative assistant to a history professor. When her handsome new boss yells at her on the first day of work, Francie worries she will never be good enough.

For Professor Alex Diederik, life is going downhill fast. Not only is his bitter ex-wife trying to poison their only daughter against him, but now his one place of solace—his work environment—is being complicated by his attractive new administrative assistant. She drives home his feelings of failure as a husband and father, and Alex wonders if hiring her was the right thing to do.

Francie will have to put aside her hurt and insecurities or risk her dreams, while Alex must look outside himself if he's to mend the breach with his daughter. And, perhaps, find someone who can help heal his pain.

One

Francie placed flowers on the grave and stepped back. Since the burial two months ago, she had come every Sunday, the only day she had off from both her jobs. She didn't really know why she still did it. Maybe it was the feeling that people who had known her and Greg would expect it. They had all thought the marriage was a good one in spite of his bad health. It had all been a lie.

At the sound of approaching footsteps, Francie glanced over her shoulder. She turned, a smile replacing her earlier frown.

"Hey, Ma," Rafe said, coming to stand beside her.

"Hi." She smiled up at her only child, feeling a powerful sense of gratitude that something good had come from Greg. Rafaele had his father's height and light eyes, but he had gotten his dark hair, olive complexion, and slender frame from her. She said a silent prayer that life wouldn't turn Rafe into the bitter, spiteful man his father had become.

"You shouldn't come here." Rafe shoved his hands in his pockets. "He didn't deserve it."

"I thought you were going to pack today." Francie wasn't going to argue with him. She had given up trying to stop Rafe from making disparaging comments about his father, but she refused to acknowledge them.

"Done. I have to talk to you though."

Something in his tone made Francie turn to face him. She crossed her arms but dropped them almost immediately. After Rafe had taken a psychology class and studied body language, he had harassed her for doing it, saying that it was a sign she was closed up. She would have reminded him that she was the parent, but his harshest comment had been that she only dropped her arms at home when she was doing something with them. Francie might have been able to keep her problems from their neighbors, but Rafe had lived the truth.

Her little protector, now all grown up.

"Let's sit down." Rafe guided her to a stone bench not far from the grave.

He sounded so serious that Francie's stomach twisted. Her biggest fear was that he would make the same mistakes she and his father had. Greg had been so handsome in his cap and gown, so confident. They were going to conquer the world, and Francie had believed every word of it. College, great jobs. They were going to have it all. She clenched her rough, callused hands and took a deep breath, trying to steel herself for bad news, clinging to Rafe's comment that he was packed.

"I don't like leaving you alone like this." He leaned forward, his hands on his knees, not looking at her. "I don't have to go, you know."

"You will stop talking nonsense." Francie shifted so she could face him, her poor heart thudding. All these years of working two jobs so he could have the best opportunities—and he might throw them away because of *her*? "Getting that scholarship to Harvard is as much my reward as yours. They don't give out many of those each year."

"You think I don't know that?" Rafe sat up, scowling. "Look, Ma—"

"No." Francie crossed her arms. "I don't need anyone's help."

"That's the problem. You've done it all for too long." Rafe jumped to his feet and strode to the grave, glaring at it. "And all those years, taking that, that—" He bit back the word and kicked at the flowers instead.

Francie let Rafe rant. Once he had calmed down—and he always did—she could reason with him. He finally gave the flowers one more kick and turned to her.

"It makes me sick to think of leaving you here alone."

"Oh, really?" She indicated the grave. "Let's be real here. It would have been easier for you to leave me alone with *him*?"

Rafe dropped onto the ground in front of the bench and ripped out a clump of grass. She slid off the seat and sat beside him, their shoulders touching. When she didn't say anything, he stopped mangling the lawn and leaned his head on her shoulder.

She blinked back sudden tears; he couldn't see her cry. Rafe could be so stubborn. If he got it in his mind that staying in Boone with her was the right thing to do, he would. Even if it meant giving back the prestigious scholarship.

"Have you decided what you're going to do?" Rafe finally asked, lifting his head.

"I have." Francie had been hoping for this question.

She reached into her purse and removed an envelope.

"What the—" Rafe said, when he read the return address. He took out the letter and gave it a quick scan. "Appalachian State? Sweet! When did you apply?"

"When you applied to Harvard. Same with the scholarships."

Rafe leapt to his feet. "You got a scholarship?"

"No scholarship for me." Francie tugged on the leg of his jeans, the ratty condition making her grimace. He was saving his new clothes for school. When he finally stopped in front of her, Rafe ran a hand through his short, dark hair. Confused by his expression, she asked, "Are you upset about this?"

"No." Rafe reached for her hands and pulled her to her feet. "I'm ticked because you didn't tell me about it sooner."

"I wasn't sure they'd accept me." Francie looked at the grave to the side. "You had enough on your mind about your own application. I didn't want you to worry about mine."

"But I thought Dad's life insurance only paid off his medical bills. How are you going to pay for your tuition?"

"I've applied for a job on campus, a full-time one." Francie reached up and straightened his hair. "If I get that, the benefit will be three quarters of my tuition. Grants will cover the rest."

"Ma." Rafe grabbed her hand and held it against his chest. "It doesn't add up. Full-time work plus full-time school plus studying? You won't have time to work a second job. How will you live?"

"Who do you think you are?" Francie jerked her hand back. "Your father?"

"Don't be insulting." Rafe's eyes flashed.

"I'm sorry. It's just that an eighteen-year-old boy

shouldn't have to be worrying about his mother."

Rafe's face softened. "We're in this together, remember? Isn't that what you've always told me? You know I won't be able to concentrate if I'm worried about whether or not you have enough food to eat and decent clothes to wear."

"See what I mean? That's *my* line." Francie picked up her purse and the letter Rafe had dropped. What would she have done all these years without him? She took his arm and led him toward her old clunker. "Look, I've got a good counselor, and she's full of ideas. Since I'm a new student I'll be taking low-level general ed. classes this first year." She sighed. "Including remedial math."

Rafe's bicycle leaned against the old Reliant K car her Granny Gladys had left Francie the year before, along with the house. The only way Francie had survived the last nineteen years had been with the old woman's quiet, unassuming help.

"You want to ride with me?" Francie asked, when Rafe pulled his helmet from the handlebars.

"No, I've got a date."

Francie forced her expression to stay neutral. She remembered what it had been like at his age. If her parents hadn't put up so much resistance to her marrying Greg, she probably wouldn't have rushed into it right after graduating from high school. Yet, looking at her tall son, Francie knew she could never regret that decision. It had given her Rafe.

"Want to take my car?" she asked with an almost-sincere smile.

Rafe put on the helmet and threw a well-muscled leg over the bar. "Really?" He gave her his typical you-didn't-just-say-that look. "*You*? On *my* bike?"

"You won't be out late, will you?"

"Love you, Ma." Rafe rode away.

Francie sighed and unlocked her door. Why hadn't she realized that her son becoming an adult didn't mean she would stop worrying about him?

Alex paused before entering the breakfast nook. Sam was already at the table, sipping a cup of herbal tea. He could tell it wasn't going to be a good day. His daughter's dark strawberry blond hair hung greasily—from product and not from a lack of hygiene—around her shoulders, highlighting the black makeup that filled the entire eye socket area. She had a light coating on her face of what had to be white greasepaint. A white lace choker accented the black, sleeveless, pseudo-leather bodice.

He closed his eyes, not wanting to see anymore. The image of the sweet little girl who had once come running to throw her arms around his neck filled his mind. That was when he had liked coming home from work. How had he screwed up so bad that Sam had turned into this? At first it had seemed harmless enough, just a weird style phase. He had assured himself that wearing Goth clothing wasn't dangerous by itself. Now, however, the extremeness of her makeup and clothes had become a barometer of her emotional stability.

Alex opened his eyes. But what did he do with this?

"Daddy, are you coming?" Sam pointed to the seat across from her.

Trying to calm his mounting frustration, Alex forced on a smile and entered the nook, pausing to kiss the top of her head. He resisted the temptation to wipe his mouth, wondering what she could have put in her hair to make it like that.

"How did you sleep?" Alex asked, opening the fridge. He took out a carton of eggs and held them for her to see, his brows raised in query.

"I don't understand how you can eat the unborn." She shuddered and took another sip of her herbal tea. The haughty disdain reminded him of his ex-wife. Divorce certainly hadn't freed him of that.

"You ate them six months ago."

"I'm enlightened now." Sam heaved a sigh, tilting her head and putting on a martyred expression. Another perfect imitation of her mother.

If he could keep them apart, he might have a chance to help Sam. He had seen *Victoria* the week before. Now that she had a rich Frenchman for a husband, she was too good for simple "Vicki." Her thinness had surprised Alex, but Sam's recent odd eating choices had become clear.

Watching his daughter from the corner of his eye, he had to fight down feelings of loathing for her mother. Not for what the woman had done to him, though that had been bad enough. He didn't usually buy into the negative energy hate generated, but watching Sam slip through his fingers. . .

"Classes start next week." Alex scooped his scrambled eggs onto a plate. "Do you have all your books?"

Sam glared at him through hooded eyes.

"So, is that a yes?"

"Sure."

"Was there enough in your account, or do I need to transfer more money in?" Alex sat at the table and stabbed a forkful of eggs.

"I didn't look."

"Samantha!" He slammed the fork on the table and scrambled eggs flew across it. Sam squealed, pushing back and knocking the last of her tea into his plate. Breathing heavily, Alex stared at the mess.

"*You* did that." Sam shot him an accusatory glare. "No way am I cleaning that disgusting stuff up." She moved as though to slide past his chair.

"Stay here." Alex grabbed her wrist. It was so small in his hand, frail almost. A stab of fear went through him. Did she have an eating disorder?

"You're hurting me, Daddy." Sam's voice was small.

He let her go and looked at her, *really* looked at her, beyond the ghastly makeup and the disaffection. Where was Sam in there? With Vicki poisoning first her mind and now her body, was he going to lose his little girl?

"Baby, I'm sorry."

"Don't call me that." She rubbed her wrist, her mouth pouting.

"We talked about that school account. If you overdraw—"

"Fine. I'll look it up and tell you if I need more money in it." Sam stomped past him.

Alex grabbed a washcloth from the sink and went to work on the table. The college semester would start in a few days. Thank heavens he would have that release. Otherwise, he might go crazy.

Francie stared at her reflection in the mirror. It hadn't been that hard getting used to Greg being gone, but Rafe's absence made the big old house seem so empty. Two months ago she had been cooking for three. Now, it was just her.

She picked up the curling iron and twisted a long strand of hair around it, considering the view of the large bedroom behind her. So many memories in this house. Good ones from when she was a child. Before Greg.

Not long after his first accident, only a couple of months after they were married, her grandmother had decided the old place was too much work and moved into a condo. Francie had been pregnant then, and Gran had insisted that she just needed someone to care for the place. In spite of the head injury, it had been something Greg could handle—until three years later, when a second car crash had put him in a wheelchair.

There was so much Francie would love to do to the graceful old house. Besides needing a new roof and fixing the dry rot along the eaves, it needed paint. Gran would die to see it now. She had worked hard to get it on Boone's official register of historic homes. It made Francie doubly sad that her beloved grandmother hadn't lived long enough to see her dream for the old place come true.

Francie turned and examined her hair. The dark strands flowed nicely down her back. In her other jobs, it hadn't been smart to look nice. Or pretty. Plain and drab meant fewer passes from creepy guys, either from the owners of the homes she cleaned or the customers at the Quick Mart.

She checked her mascara. The makeup had turned out well that morning. It was a good thing she had decided to practice Saturday. It had been so long since she had worn makeup that her first try had made her look like a student from the Mimi Bobeck School of Makeup Artistry. After practicing a couple of days, Francie had finally been happy with the results.

She tipped up her heel. The black pumps, though from Goodwill, were cute and almost new. They were the first heels she had worn in years, and she hadn't been able to resist the red sole. Especially after she had found the beautiful, secondhand suit with the red blouse. It was so classy, and the price so affordable, that Francie had kept looking over her shoulder, expecting someone to tell her there had been a mistake. Starting a new life, she wanted to try something different.

Stepping back from the mirror, she did a full figure check. She didn't recognize herself. How could a used outfit and some cheap makeup make her look so much younger?

Francie picked up the older model smart phone a friend had given her and activated the camera. Pointing it at the mirror, she snapped a selfie and sent it in a message to Rafe.

Look at the old girl now.

U better carry a gun with u Ma! Ethan asked if ur my sister. Haha

Francie already liked Rafe's Harvard roommate, Ethan, who had been present for the first online talk with her son. She had been worried Rafe might end up with someone from a rich family who had attended an Eastern prep school and would look down at a scholarship boy from North Carolina. But Ethan was from Montana and the stepson of a rancher. The young man's rough hands, tanned face, and sun-streaked sandy hair hinted at hard work.

haha

Good luck today, Ma.

Francie was glad now she had agreed to let Rafe add her to his phone plan. Knowing she could text him made it seem like he wasn't so far away. She checked her purse again. The last thing she needed to do was forget something. Her first class was right after work. Grabbing the car keys, she hurried out the door.

The car wouldn't start.

If you enjoyed this chapter and would like to read more, *Second Chances 101* can be found at:

Amazon.com

www.ingramcontent.com/pod-product-compliance
Lightning Source LLC
Chambersburg PA
CBHW060936120626
46557CB00003B/1023